IN THE SHADOW OF THE PHOSPHOROUS DAWN

ROB
TRUE

IN THE SHADOW OF THE PHOSPHOROUS DAWN

Influx Press
London

PUBLISHED BY INFLUX PRESS
THE GREENHOUSE
49 GREEN LANES, LONDON, N16 9BU
WWW.INFLUXPRESS.COM / @INFLUXPRESS
ALL RIGHTS RESERVED.
© ROB TRUE, 2021

FIRST EDITION 2021. PRINTED AND BOUND IN THE UK BY TJ BOOKS.

PAPERBACK ISBN: 9781910312711
EBOOK ISBN: 9781910312728

EDITOR: GARY BUDDEN
COPYEDITOR: DAN COXON
PROOFREADER: TRUDI SHAW
COVER DESIGN: VINCE HAIG
INTERIOR DESIGN: VINCE HAIG

For my Elena

CARL ON A BENCH IN THE MIDDAY SUN. A FLY LANDS ON HIS HAND – it looks like the hand of a dead man. Pale, yellow skin, purple blotch of decay. He watches the fly's erratic, mechanical movement, metallic-green robot spy. A sense of doom falls across him, obscuring his thoughts in a shade of unknown horror. The day ahead of him. A looming, long, lonely day. As though, at any moment, something terrible is about to happen. Constant fear.

The sun throws its rays all over the park and Carl squints through his sunglasses. Watching a small boy playing in the grass with his mother looking on. He thinks of all the beatings the old man gave him.

The boy, playing happily, unaware of the life that awaits him. He stops, struck still by the sight of his own shadow, as though he hasn't noticed it before. There is fear on his face, and for a moment he stares down at the dark spectre. He turns away and flees, whimpering in fear. Carl watches the little boy trying to outrun his shadow, twisting this way and that, looking back as the black monster keeps up. He can't escape it. The dark figure on the floor bears down on him and the little boy cries out in panic. Carl sees the despair in the little boy's eyes. His mother sees it all and sits unmoved, a sly grin on her lips.

Carl feels it deep. He looks up to the blue above and the dark cloud moving across it. On the field, blackness creeps across the grass towards him. It fills his heart and consumes him. He stands up and walks away, turning back for one last glance at the good-looking young mother with her child. Sat on the bench, short skirt, nice legs, but the darkness moves over her. It drowns him and pretty girls won't help. There's no hope.

The woman looks him in the eye. A look of interest, but it changes to a mocking sneer. A knowing smirk. She can sense his unreasonable fear and knows his weakness. Knows he is afraid. He's no better than her snivelling toddler. She looks away, unimpressed.

Above, birds circle the sky. Rattle of magpie call scratches the day and a crow pecks at dead flesh. Silhouette hunters swoop on the rec below, where parcels of pleasure and pain are passed.

As Carl nears the street, he pauses to look back. Cloud shadow travels over the park and where he'd sat is shaded in gloom. He turns back to sun street haze and walks on.

•

The morning had got off to a strange start. Carl's brother had come back to life. Dean's wife had shown up causing trouble again. He'd told her about herself and she'd driven away screaming. Carl woke up crying. Dean was still dead. When you hang yourself, you stay dead. Wiping the tears from his face, he briefly considered ending his brother's wife. And he woke again, startled by the peace in his flat.

Thinking about last night, Carl laughed. He'd drank to his brother with his sister and his father. It had been six months. Kate had found an old bottle of Cognac in the back of a cupboard, unopened. The old man thought it was shit.

– Never heard of it. Someone give it me when you was a boy. Can't remember who.

Camus Napoleon Cognac. They cracked it open and it was beautiful. Went down like silk. The bottle was written in French. No alcohol volume, none of the legal information. Kate looked it up on the www. A rare Cognac, bottled in the seventies. The cheapest she could find it was two hundred and fifty quid. The old man, broke as fuck in an ex-council house.

– Story o' my fuckin' life. Oh well. A good drink for Dean.

•

In the cafe, Carl orders egg, bacon and tomatoes, toast and a cuppa. The young girl with a smile-mask writes down the order and pours the tea.

– Don't cut the toast.

– No, I remember. Where's your brother?

Carl has to tell the story again. How many times? He almost chokes on his words. The mask breaks and the waitress cries. Eating his food with the fog of a shattered mind, emptiness of stolen thoughts, staring into nothing. Smell of fried food. Tinkling of spoon in a mug. Finishing his tea, he looks at the paper on the table and sees an article about brutal gangland killings, wonders if it's anyone he knows.

Fucking morons knocking each other off.

Paying for his food and the girl, so sad.

– I'm so sorry for you. Your brother was nice.

– Thank you.

Outside, the road deserted. Like a mystic dream road, empty parked cars, strange silence. Bleak street, desolate heart. Grey, melancholy sky. He walks back to a lonely black van.

The client is already there when he gets to the car park. Carl pulls up in the space next to her car. Greek bird. Husband at it. So she said. Just needs the evidence. These lot are all the same. A bit wealthy. Bored wives, or husbands doing too much overtime. Wanting to catch their cheating spouse in the act.

He gets out and greets her, detached manner. Some of the women try it on a bit. Flick of the hair, flirty eyes. Show a bit of leg.

– Did you listen to it?

– Never do. None of my business what's on it. You pay me and I hand it over.

Nobody wants to pay for a recording of nothing.

– How much is it again?

– Two hundred.

She gives him the dough and he passes her the recording. Easy money. Give the client a bug to place somewhere to catch a betrayal. Park a motor outside with a voice-activated recorder. Leave for twenty-four hours. Collect, get paid, pass over the evidence. As many days as they want. They do most of the work themselves. He can still do small building jobs, refurbs, kitchens. He could work when he wanted. As little as possible. Carl was never a fan of hard work. He hated the thought of devoting his life to it. He was still trying to get used to being a part of it all. Society, life, the way things are. Having to fit in somehow.

TRYING TO RELAX IN A BATH, CARL FEELS THE WATER TIGHTEN ON his skin. Each bubble a universe of rainbow horror. He hates soap. Hates the artificial smell. The feeling of it shrinking on his flesh. Itching. The internal dialogue of a jumbled mind. Thoughts racing with a strange and twisted understanding, then lost in rambling disorder. Confusion of thoughts obliterated. Unable to slow down or hold on to any meaningful idea, Carl sinks his head below the surface. He sees himself, covered in blood, screaming silently. Eyes on fire. Chaos wells up, like an explosion building inside. He comes up for air to a still room, atmosphere of trepidation and the thoughts still racing, like a film on fast-forward. Carl feels a presence at the door ajar. A feeling of being watched. Looking up, he sees an eye at the crack, peeping. Cold creeps through his bones.

– Hello?

The dark figure moves away.

– Who's there?

Nothing. There's nobody else in the flat. He wonders if he is even really there himself. Shadow spreading out from the coved corner of the bathroom ceiling, reaching slow darkness of eclipse. Fear bloom in the gut, like smoke clouds billowing, billowing, billowing.

•

In the living room now; Carl wonders how he got there. He remembers the bath and then nothing. From that moment to the next in another room, hours later. No memory of what occurred between. Blank.

He picks up the paper. Strange gangland killings.

Unexplained deaths of villains. Police, no leads. Unusual deaths. Details leaked. Blunt trauma, followed by the removal of the heart, while victims are still alive. Hearts are missing. Murders look like savage attacks, ending with bizarre ritual sacrifices. Not what you'd expect from criminals bumping each other off. Usually done by shooting or stabbing. Sometimes it's torture. But not like this.

Door entry buzz of shattered peace and broken mind intrusion of outside coming in. Carl goes to the hallway and talks into the entry-phone receiver.

– Hello?

– It's me.

– Anna?

– Who else? Let me in.

Carl presses the button and hears the buzz and the heavy slam, then landing silence broken by the echo of high heels on stairs. He waits by the door, listening. The click of heels falls nearer and the door bangs. Carl looks through the spyhole, unsure if it will be Anna, or some trick played on him. It is her. He opens the door.

– Alright?

– I'm alright, what about you? What's the matter? Did you forget I was coming?

– Na, I just lost track of time.

– Again? You keep saying that. Did you forget what you were doing?

– I don't know. Must've nodded off.

Carl watches Anna hang her coat and put her bag down. Bending over, her skirt goes up, teasing at the top of her thighs just below the swell of her cheeks.

– You should go to the doctor. You keep forgetting stuff.

He puts his hand gently round her throat and gripping the windpipe, shoves her against the wall, lifting her onto her toes.

– Shh. Your heels rise for me.

Her face softens in a look of lust, eyebrows arch. He kisses her deep, lowering her back onto high heels, and lets go of her neck. Anna unzips her skirt and drops it with her underwear. She steps out of her knickers and stares defiantly, eyes alight.

– I haven't got time for your games.

– I ain't got time for your lip.

Carl takes her arm and twists it up behind her back, grabs a handful of hair and frogmarches her to the living room. He pushes her over the sofa arm, face down, arse up, and kicks her legs apart.

•

Watching telly, aftermath bliss of fuck-dream-daze. Anna smoking and telling Carl about her day. The news is on and Carl sits forward to turn up the volume. The story about the murdered criminals.

– Have you seen this?

– Yeah. Anyone we know?

– Dunno. Old Bill are trying to keep it hushed, but some little fucker leaked the gory details to the papers. No names though.

– You seen any of that lot?

– I told ya, I'm done with all them lot.

– Alright. You just seem a bit preoccupied lately. You keep losing time.

– I broke all my ties. I ain't lying.

– You can't blame me for asking. You don't seem right to me. Go to the doctor. You've been through a lot of stress.

– I'll be alright when me brain chemistry settles down.

– I know, but on top of that, you've had your brother 'n all that. Just go and see someone. It can't hurt. You never talk about it.

– I don't want to talk about it.

– Suit yourself. I worry about you, Carl.

PAPA LOU GETS OUT OF THE BLACK BENZ AND WALKS TO A RED FRONT door. The Hunter watches 'til the last moment. Already knows there's nobody else there. Papa Lou pushes the door open. The Hunter, out from the shadows, creeps under a mad moon in predator steps of cold calm. Papa Lou turns to see, holds down the jump and stays cool.

– Come.

He turns back into the doorway and The Hunter follows. Across the threshold, pulls the sawn-off head of a lump hammer from jacket pocket, swings it into temple. A sickening *crack* and The Hunter slams the door behind them as Papa Lou goes down, kufi skidding on the tiled floor. The Hunter removes a long coat, shoves it in a plastic bag and throws it to the corner by the stairs. Standing over prone man, snarling, fire through blood, like magic. Mind swimming in mad soup. One more hit for luck, a dull thud and Papa Lou lies stunned as The Hunter strips him. Shoes first, trousers and underwear yanked down and off, followed by socks. Shirt pulled open and sleeves tugged from arms. The big man nude, The Hunter kneels down by the moaning flesh on the floor. Blood mess from the head and face, lips opening and closing, no sound. Papa Lou struggles and grabs the smaller figure, but he is weak from the head injury and falls limp from three hard punches.

The Hunter pulls a knife, drags sharp shiv across dark skin under bone cage, spilling red. Open cavern, hand in up to the forearm, warm viscera, finds pumping muscle and pulls out.

Mad beat of held heart, as The Hunter bites into pulsing core and claret everywhere. Consumes the heart and feels the gold light come in, like a beam from heaven.

Transformed into a god. Magician with a baboon head. The golden glow flow in the blood and The Hunter hisses like a cat as the power throbs through veins. The monster stands and roars, head thrown back, blood mouth bubbling. Visions of wild beasts killing and eating each other, an orgy of cannibalism. Sees its own face in the mirror change into a mask, malevolent grin of death and hunger. Ecstasy.

The Hunter standing over a red-soaked bathtub, washing away blood, has no idea what the time is. Rinses the tub with shower head and wipes taps and everything touched. Walks back to hallway horror of smashed skull, open torso, and pulls the coat on. Rolls up the bloodstained T-shirt and puts it in the carrier bag. Driving across town to an estate with communal bins. Nobody about. The Hunter dumps the bag with the T-shirt and drives into the dream night, mad moon, cut like a peephole in the black above. Street lights blur and trail a strange orange glow on enchanted concrete vision.

CARL IN THE PARK, SITTING ON A TREE STUMP STARING AT NOTHING. Grey clouds move fast above, give an impression the sky is leaving. Something bursts inside him. He looks down to silent movement of green blades and the grass blows a rhythm of waves. Smell of fields and the sound of a warm breeze. An abrupt awareness of being watched rudely interrupts Carl's state of peace and he looks up at the large shrub in front of him. Is there someone behind it spying on him? No, it's the bush watching him. Knowing. Seeing it all, deep inside. All the secrets too. All the pain, the lies, a frightened boy, through shoddy disguise of cool front, no cares and unafraid of anyone. Terrible moment of frozen bone fear in the marrow and burning through blood, as the bush takes on ominous aura of enemy entity. The air turns solid around him. Carl sits still, looking at the malevolent shrub expanding, as it looks back defiant, menacing atmosphere. He feels like something bad is going to occur.

His attention is caught by a dark cloud in the blue above, moving a sly shadow across him. He gets up to leave, but it's too late. Two men sit down on a bench by the path. They look at Carl and he thinks they might be somehow involved with the watching bush. He walks back to the van, looks around, gets in and drives away.

Nothing was going on back there.

– Nothing was going on back there.

Carl says it out loud and repeats it several times.

You're an idiot.

– Fuck off!

He raps his head with his knuckles.

TWO NUDE GIRLS TWIRL ON A STAGE, KISS AND SWAY. WIND THEIR HIPS. Lit bright, super trooper beam in the gloom. Slow, seductive dance. Audience dark, unlit. Sitting at small tables. Shadow faced. Anonymous. Mesmerised. Pretty waitresses bring them drinks. Anna watches the dance. Another girl finishes counting up the till. Anna goes behind the bar to stand with her.

– Good night tonight?

– Not bad.

– All alright then?

– Yeah, all good. Nothing out of order.

The bouncers step aside to allow a group of men through the door. Anna watches them walk through and stand at the back in the shadows. Ominous presence. Several large men. Anna recognises one of the silhouettes as Mick. He nods at her and she waves back.

The show finishes as the spotlights darken and the girls leave the stage. The dim wall lights brighten. A tall woman appears at the centre and announces the end of the night. The audience cheer and whistle.

– Thank you for coming, I hope you enjoyed the show. Please make your way out of the building.

The guests slowly stand and shuffle out into the night. Five men at the back remain standing. A waitress brings them drinks. Anna takes the cash from the girl at the till, walks to a door at the side and goes into the small room behind it. She opens a safe and puts the money in it.

Mick and his entourage walk over to the door. Mick knocks.

– Come in.

The men all go in. Anna is standing at a desk with the five men crowded around her in the small room. The men are all staring at her. Mick steps closer.

– I promised the lads a girl tonight.

Anna looks at Mick. She is wary of his close proximity and being surrounded in the small room, but doesn't show it. Relaxed face, cool smile.

– I'll fetch some of the girls. They can choose.

– They've already chosen.

Anna looks round at the smiling faces. Leering grins. There's no way out. The big man by the door pushes it shut and locks it.

•

At home, Carl looking out the window, trying to remember how he got there. Calm stillness of quiet flat. The sky turns mauve and breaks up into patterns. As he stares through it, the small fragments spread out from the window frame into the room with him, and Carl sits there watching them dance and turn in the air around him. He looks at the space before him and the furniture is just visible through the jumbled shapes of colour. The pattern fades out and the room fades in, clear, as though it had always been there, without interruption. Carl feels out of place. Like he's just appeared in an alien world. Odd and awkward, a sense of foreboding. A distant telephone rings in the quiet. A door slams somewhere in the block. Then peace again.

Silence shattered by buzz of telecom, every cell on edge, and Carl answers with a hatred of everything outside of him.

– Hello.

– Open the door.

– Who's that?

– It's Mick. Open the fuckin' door.

What does he fuckin' want?

Carl reluctantly presses the buzzer and waits. As he hears the footsteps approach, it's clear there are at least two people, maybe more, and Carl feels doom coming his way. He looks through the spyhole and in the corner of the landing, a shadow spreads across the floor towards his door. Mick's face appears with two others behind. Tom and Frank.

What's he got them pair'a cunts with him for?

The door bangs.

– Open up, ya prick.

Carl turns the door handle and Mick shoves it into him and pushes past.

– Alright, Mick?

– No. Do I look happy?

– Dunno. What's up? Hello boys.

Tom and Frank don't reply and stare Carl down.

– What's up? I heard you've been snooping around.

– What d'ya mean?

– Take 'im in there, I don't like standing in the hall.

Tom grabs Carl's arm and steers him into the living room. Carl's flesh prickles at the atmosphere and he knows it's not a friendly visit.

– Sit down.

Carl sits, aided by an encouraging shove, and the other three men stand over him. They distort, growing in size before him. Features enlarged. Square faced. Heavy brow, predator eyes.

– Now what's all this I hear about you snooping?

– I dunno what you're on about, Mick.

Carl is trying to think what he's done to invite this unwelcome visit. Perhaps he has spied on a friend of Mick's.

– Don't fuckin' lie to me, cause I'll hurcha. A little birdie told me that you were snoopin' on naughty girls and boys playing away.

– Oh that? Yeah, well, you know. I gotta eat, ain't I?

– So you're a dirty little snooper then, ain't ya?

Carl shrugs a nod.

– So, Snoopy. You got buggin' devices, right?

– Yeah. That's all I do. I just record and sell 'em the recording.

Mick rubs his chin and looks out the window thoughtfully. He turns back and smacks Carl in the face with a hammer-fist.

– Ah, what's that for?

– When you stopped doing work with me, I thought, I'll keep an eye on that one. Never know what the mad little cunt'll do next. But I heard you got yourself straightened out and I'm thinking, he's done alright. But now look. Now you gone and got yourself in trouble, ain't ya?

– Why?

– Why? I don't know why. That's just how it goes, son. You can't escape yourself, can you? You know what your biggest fuckin' problem is?

– What?

– You're seein' it every time you look in the mirror, son. It's you. You can't get away from you. Have you seen the news, the killin's?

– Yeah. What's it all about?

– Fuck knows. Nobody knows. Two of ours, three Africans, a couple of Yard boys, a few Turks, five of the blacks down the way, one of the Pakis. Even the Irish. No one knows who's doin' it. All blamin' each other. The Old Bill don't know nothin'. Ain't got a clue.

– What are you gonna do?

– No, what are *you* gonna do? That's what you should be askin'.

– Why?

– You're goin' back to work, son.

– No, I'm done.

– Don't you fuckin' tell me what's what. I'm tellin' *you*. You're the one who worked with everybody. You're the lone ranger. You're the fuckin' Snoopy. I tell you what you're gonna do. You're goin' back to work with everyone. You're going to use your little nosey devices and stick your snoopin' snout into everything and find out what's fuckin' happenin'. What's the matter? You don't look keen.

– I don't want to get involved.

– Tom.

Tom leans over and punches Carl in the side of the head. Frank drags him out of his seat and holds him while Tom gives him a few digs. Frank lets go and Carl crumples and folds up on the floor. Mick puts his foot on Carl's face and pushes down with all his weight, crushing him into the floor. Carl resists the urge to fight back. He can't win.

– You're gonna do it, or you're gonna get it. Understand?

– Yes.

– Good. Now, here's a little treat to get you back into the swing of things.

Mick lifts his foot off Carl's cheek and signals to Frank. Frank chucks a bag of light brown powder on the floor, next to Carl's face.

– Don't do it all at once.

When he hears the footsteps getting quieter on the stairs, Carl pulls himself up and wipes the blood across his mouth.

– Cunts.

He picks up the bag of powder and throws it at the door. He tries to think through the blurred haze of a punched head. Blank mind of stress-broken thought and no answers come. No way out. He gets up and walks over to the little bag. Looks about a quarter. He picks it up and lobs it in the bin and sits down on the sofa. Then he gets up again and fishes it out the bin and puts it in a drawer, slams it shut. He sits down and puts his head in his hands.

– Fuck sake.

Carl looks up to the ceiling and holds his hands stretched out, like Jesus on the cross.

– I'm tryin'. I'm really tryin' hard. Can't you just toss me something good? Anything?

He drops his arms by his sides, still looking up.

– Cunt.

THE BUZZER GOES AND CARL'S HEART BEATS HARDER. HE GOES TO answer.

What now?

– Hello?

– It's me.

Carl buzzes Anna in, opens the door and sits back down in the living room. He hears the door close and Anna walks in.

– What happened to your face?

– Had a fight.

– Looks like you lost.

– You should see the other fellas.

– How many?

– Three.

Carl leans forward, clutching his trunk.

– Are you alright?

– I think they've bruised me ribs.

– What's going on, Carl? There's something up with you, what is it?

– Nothing. Just got in a fight, that's all.

Anna gives Carl a look of uncertainty and he knows she isn't convinced. She sits on the sofa with her legs open, so he can see up her skirt. No knickers.

– Well, are you going to fuck me then, or what? Do you think I come here to look after you when you get a beating? If you're not up to it, I'm going home.

Carl watches her face distort and grow, as it melts away to reveal a monstrous mask of possession. It alters again, and she is beautiful. Soft glow in the gloom around them. A terrible angel. The light is inside or behind her. Some message he can't understand. Those eyes of fire. Carl stares at her soft-focus face. She has a halo.

●

Getting dressed, Anna looks at Carl, questioning gaze of knowing there's something more than what she's been told. Carl keeps his eyes to himself, not wanting to give it up. He knows his windows are open to her and she can look right through into his bone-box and the pictures in there are hers to be seen. There is a magic about her; everything is hers for the taking. He wishes he was wearing sunglasses. He knows she can tell he is trying not to look at her.

– There's something you're not telling me, Carl. I'm not going to push it, but I want you to understand. I'm not hanging around for you to get fucked up again.

– Alright, I know. I'm okay.

– Good. Stay that way.

– Listen, you've had your dirty way with me, now can ya fuck off so I can get on with it.

– Where are you going?

– I told ya. I got to meet a client. Who's got no memory now?

DRIVING OUT THE CAR PARK, SUN LOW IN THE SKY AND THE WHOLE scene shimmering and unreal. Gold glare reflected in windows on the block, and the houses across the way are black against heaven aflame in the blue. Dark shadow across the quarter-light, over tarmac and still cars parked, like a figure looming. Shadow snide. Carl drives out into the road.

A man jumps out in front of the car, arms outstretched, and he roars through a paper-bag mask, face drawn on in felt tip. Carl slams on the anchors and stares at the man crossing in front of him, like nothing had happened. Nothing is real. He pulls out onto the main road.

Rising on the horizon, stark monolith against the dusk. One of three. Many eyes of gold ablaze. Sheer face, home to falcon, preys on the rec below. Tintagel House. Home to the broke and busted. To drunks, addicts and lonely mothers. To lost losers and lunatics.

Puddle of piss in the lift, twenty-three floors up. Bang on the door. Carl stands there, aware of being looked at through a spyhole. Five separate locks are loudly opened and the door swings in.

– Yes, bless, come in.

– Easy, blue.

– What's up, blood? How you doin'?

– Alright, geezer, alright.

– Come through.

– Cheers.

Five men sitting about, smoking weed. Heavy lids, red eyes. Carl nods, but nobody responds. Ten eyes staring through him. Eighties décor and green velvet furniture. Dub playing on a sound system. Thick smoke hangs in the room.

– So, you couldn't keep away, blood. I heard you finished with this business.

– Yeah, well. A man's gotta eat, ain't he?

– Yeah, yeah. True.

Carl scanning for somewhere to hide the bug, with five people watching. He avoids eye contact.

– Ya wan' three boxes?

– Yeah, mate.

Carl pulls the cash out and puts it on the table, as he drops the listening device on the carpet.

– This gear is crazy, blood.

– Your thing's always good.

– Better than good.

Carl kicks the bug under a sofa. It doesn't go all the way under, so he kicks it again.

– Yeah, man.

One of the men on the sofa says something, Carl doesn't catch.

– What did you say?

– Who's talking to you?

The man kisses his teeth and stares at Carl with menace.

Carl looks away as Clarence puts the last parcels in a carrier bag.

Clarence walks Carl to the door.

– What's his problem?

– Don't worry 'bout 'im.

– It's him should be worried about me.

– He's a bad man.

– So what? He's gonna look fuckin' bad when I'm done with 'im.

– Take it easy.

– See ya later, geezer.

Carl goes down to his van to get the receiver. Back in the lift, stink of piss, as he stands in a dry corner. The lift gets smaller. He sits in the van a while, to pass time. He goes back to the block and waits for somebody to come out, so he can get back in. Back up in the lift to twenty-second floor, then up the stairs to twenty-third floor so no one hears the lift arrive. On the landing, Carl listens for noise, looking at Clarence's door. Nothing. He reaches up and pushes aside a square ceiling tile. He places the recorder above the drop ceiling.

THE DRAWER CATCHES AND JAMS AS HE PULLS IT AND CARL SLAMS IT shut and tries again. It opens freely this time and there it is. A little bag of light brown powder. He picks it up and turns it in his hand. A terrible feeling goes through his blood and the heat in his face makes him sweat. The air is thick around him. He puts it back and shuts the drawer.

I gotta get rid of it.

Carl takes a white brick from one bag and puts it in another.

Out by the van and a shadow cast on the block, moving slow. Carl lobs the bag in the back, looks up to grey clouds, shadow looming, and gets in and turns the engine over. He pulls away, checking mirrors. The shadow snide follows and he speeds up. Pulling out onto the main road, traffic backed up, football match with hooligan reputation of fear. Heavy police presence. Carl don't mind the jam. Police busy herding. They got their hands full. He thinks of his brother and sees him hanging. Stereo playing Chas 'n' Dave's 'Ain't No Pleasing You'. He listens to the lyrics and thinks of his poor brother's doomed marriage. A tear runs down his face. Sweet death hits him in the gut with a sinking drop of nowhere-tumble into the abyss. His brother's face smiles at him through melancholy twilight. The hanged man takes on Carl's face and he sees himself swinging, a smile on his lips, thinking of peace and no more fuss, no stress. No more torment. Death gives you silence.

Release me.

•

At Jim's place, tidy house. Open plan. Nothing out of place. Like a show home. Thick carpet, sickly smell of air freshener, perfume and cooking. Everything bland and fashionable. Lisa making something in the kitchen.

– You alright, love?

– Yeah, can't complain. You?

– Alright. You wanna cuppa?

– Na, I'm in a hurry, thanks.

Carl puts the bag on the table, while Jim counts out the paperwork.

– How you been keeping?

– Yeah, alright.

– Back at it?

– Yeah, mate.

– Seen all them killin's?

– Yeah, man. No one knows who's done 'em, do they?

– Na. I heard it was Yard boys.

– Who told ya that? Couple'a theirs got done 'n all.

– Yeah. True. But that don't mean nothing. There was some weird voodoo shit involved.

– Yardies just rob people, mate. They don't do magic. I ain't havin' that.

– Sorry to hear about your brother, mate.

– Yeah. Cheers.

Jim walks out to the hall and Carl puts a bug behind the dresser.

– How 'ave you been copin'?

Lisa tries to sound sympathetic and Carl feels uncomfortable. Lisa looks like she's made of plastic. A robot, or some kind of puppet. She tries to make small talk and Carl wishes Jim would come back quick. Jim walks into the room with more money and they finish counting it out.

DAYS AND NIGHTS OF LISTENING TO NOTHING. ON AND ON. Recordings of deals and gossip and who grassed up who and so-and-so's a wanker and crack pipes crackling, lighters lighting and nothing at all and so on and so on. And Carl bored, wishing it wasn't him who had to do it, but no way out without repercussions. Recording droning on in background noise of disembodied voices. Smoke rising. Lost concentration. The recording disappearing into nonsense noise. Words lose meaning. Shadow spreading out from the corner of the room. Darkness reaching out towards him, slow stretching shadow fingers and Carl feeling a terrible doom, with the voices, monotonous, meaningless words. Shadow man in the corner, pointing, reaching out. Visions of hanged man, poor brother swinging, stretched neck. Death. More murders, no leads. Carl in the void, nowhere-dream, shadows looming. He opens a bottle of dark rum. Takes a long hit.

– Dean.

He thinks of his brother. Hard as nails, funny as fuck.

Why did you do that?

There's no reason for anything, Carl knows that. It's all a con. A lie. A meaningless game and Dean bailed. He'd had enough. Dean would have fought back when Mick's boys knocked Carl about. Wouldn't have done him any good though. The only way to beat people like Mick is killing them. Dean had a reckless violence about him. Didn't care if a man was weak or powerful, or of any consequence. Prison, or death. Dean never thought of these things when his blood was up. Carl had more instinct for survival. If fighting meant surviving, he'd fight. If *not* fighting meant surviving, he'd accept his small humiliation. Considering the outcomes, Carl played with the idea of not investigating. He knew he was in for a kicking, or worse if he didn't come up with any result. At least he had some recordings to show, however useless. It wasn't his fault if nobody talked about who'd done the killings. There's no such thing as fate. It's all an accident. Chance. If Mick had a heart attack in his sleep tonight, he could leave it all behind. Carry on as if nothing had happened.

TURNING THE BAG OVER IN HIS HAND. FEEL OF SOFT POWDER THROUGH thin plastic. A strange sensation of the forbidden. Like having an affair.

I'll put it in the muscle just in case. Not used to it now, but what does it matter anyway. Who cares? Me dad, me sister, Anna? They're better off without me.

– Anna thinks you're a cunt.

– Fuck off.

– Everyone thinks you're scum. Weak.

– Leave me alone.

Carl rubs his hand over his face, dragging the skin. He laughs at nothing and then laughs again, hysterical.

Bag open, spoon, water, syringe. Fizz of cooking, brown spreading in clear fluid. The filter soaks it up. Drawn into the barrel with a rising anticipation of morphine memory. Pierce flesh, blood bloom. Gentle injection in the thigh. A warmth radiating from the back of the head. Brown bliss, kiss of God. Carl on the sofa nodding out. Soft focus dim room, emptiness of a silent mind. Broken moments in lost time. Here and there. Somewhere else. Opiate dream for soul eclipsed, blurred fuzz and fear dissolved. Heaven in a deep void. Nothing matters. Quiet of empty rooms. Nowhere. A child crying far away in another flat, as though from a different dimension, or time. Carl is a ghost again.

You can't escape your own darkness, can you?

A shadow rises from the corner, a dark figure looms in the gloom. A spectre reaches unsolid fingers of obscure touch. The shadow caresses Carl's face.

– You can't escape yourself, can you?

A small boy tries to outrun his own shadow, turning this way and that, panic rising. The boy changes direction and the shadow bears down on him, catches him. The little boy screams.

ANNA IS TALKING, BUT THE WORDS ARE JUST SOUND FROM A LONG WAY off. Carl looks at her. He can see her, but as though he is watching through a screen; he can only view her through a portal, like seeing her on telly. A tear between two separate dimensions. She fades to nothing, then reappears.

– Why are you staring at me like that?

– Eh?

– You're acting really strange.

– Am I?

She looks at him through narrowed eyes.

– Have you been using?

– Na.

– Are you alright?

– Yeah.

They kiss and then put their arms around each other. They stay like that for a long time, cheek to cheek, then Anna pulls away. Carl staring into nothing, through a no-hope wall. Anna side-eying him, aware of some sort of deviance. She doesn't want to press too much. Doesn't want to spoil what they haven't got. She puts the kettle on. Carl watches. He likes Anna and wants to open his heart to her, but he can't. He is afraid of her. She has a strange magic. It would be easy to get lost in a love that will twist his soul and distort his mind. He would fuck it all up with his darkness and she would leave him to his own torment. To destroy himself. Again. She is a lovely monster making tea. He knows that a girl like that will destroy him, no matter how much love there is. And he, too, would ruin her. She can't help it any more than he can. It's just the way it is.

– You hear about Jim?

– Na.

– Lisa found him a few days ago. Heart torn out. Same as the others.

– Fuckinell. I only seen 'im the other day. Poor Lisa.

– That beautiful thick, cream carpet must have been ruined. Poor Lisa.

– Yeah. I can't believe it.

– ANY GOOD?

– Yeah mate. This'll sort ya right out.

Carl gives the bag to John. John takes it and opens it. He scrapes some dust from the block, sets up a line and sniffs it, brings his head up sharp.

– Yeah, that hits the spot.

John stands swaying, fidgeting fingers. His left eye twitching.

– I gotta have a shit. Paperwork's on the table.

– I'll see meself out.

– Laters.

As John leaves the room, Carl looks around. Sparse flat. Not much there. Bedroom, bathroom and living room. In the living room, a couple of chairs, low fifties-style coffee table and TV on a stand. The chairs have tall legs. Nowhere good to hide the listening device. He puts a bug under the TV stand.

•

Walking back to the van under a yellow moon cut like a crooked smile in the sky, Carl sees the man from Clarence's flat. The bad man. Mad rush of blood. Adrenal toxic. Bad man staring Carl down as the gap closes, kiss of teeth. Intimidation, stare of violence. Carl looks away, like he doesn't care, then turns back and punches the bad man in the side of the head as they pass each other. A good one. Right in the temple. A loud bang echoes between the blocks of flats. Like a big empty box dropped on the floor. Bad man folds and Carl follows with three more digs as bad man tries to shield his head. Carl catches him in the ribs as he goes down, grabs him by the throat and slams the man to the floor, cracks the back of his head on concrete slab.

– Bad man yeah? You're a fuckin' pussy, man.

Five heavy fists in the face and he gets up, blood-mess shining in the melancholy moonlight and street lamp glow and the buildings around them shudder in the sad night. Carl spits on the floor, next to the battered man's head, gets up and carries on to the van, without looking back.

Letting the water out the bath, Carl wonders why he hasn't heard one clue to who's behind the killings. Nobody has said a word to give the game away. The murders seem unreal. Like a supernatural conspiracy, to remove the hearts of these criminals. A ghost is carrying out the killings. Some sort of spectre. A shadow man. What does it mean?

Carl watches the water go down the plughole and feels his life draining out with it, spinning as it goes. You just can't win. He has a meeting with Mick tomorrow. Knows it could be painful. There's nothing he can do. In his mind he scrambles for leverage. Some illusion of control. Nothing. The same desolate feeling of helplessness as he felt when he found out his brother had hanged himself, or when his mother and father beat him as a child. Nowhere. Fear hits him deep. A cold grip on his heart and the beat stops and it feels like a rock, heavy and hard in his chest. A shadow spreads out along the wall. A dark figure rises, points at Carl and a long finger stretches out towards his forehead. He can't remember the rest of the day before his bath.

•

The TV is telling Carl about a bombing in the Middle East. People crying. Dust all over everything. On the people. Then a flood somewhere. Floating debris. More dead people. More crying. It doesn't matter. So much suffering. None of it matters. All the murder, torture, starvation, disease, disaster. Over and over, back through time. It don't matter. We're all going to die. Most of us in some horrible way. The newsreader appears and speaks to him directly. She looks at him out through the screen. Her eyes turn black and bore into him.

– Kill yourself. You are scum. Kill yourself.

– Fuck off.

Carl reaches for the remote and switches it off. The screen turns blank and mirrors the room. A dark figure sits next to him on the sofa. Fear wells up from the gut as the marrow moves in his bones and he has to fight a feeling of paralysis to twist in his seat, and no one's there of course. He can still sense a presence. Carl gets up and goes to the drawer. It's empty. Remembering hiding small amounts in the light switch before, he gets a screwdriver. He undoes the faceplate and there it is. A dull feeling of security flows through him, like coming back to somewhere familiar after being lost. It masks fear and he knows he's close to home. He cooks himself a fix and gently injects some peace of mind. It all melts away, sitting there, nodding out. The fear, the stress, the shadows, all dissolves in brown liquid tranquillity.

AT LLOYD'S, THE ATMOSPHERE THICK WITH A STRANGE MALICE, AND Carl finds the temperament catching. How do you bug someone who thinks his radio is already bugged? Carl remembers Lloyd telling him his toenails were bugged and planning to tear them off with a pair of pliers. Lloyd passes the glass with a bone to smoke and grins at Carl through cracked lips and dirty, brown teeth, several missing. Mad eyes of nowhere seeing. Everywhere. Carl wonders if Lloyd has become suspicious of his teeth.

– Na mate, I'm alright.

Lloyd puts his finger to his lips and points at the window.

Carl wants to get out, but Lloyd, in a trance, leaves the room.

– Lloyd, I gotta go, man.

– I'm havin' a shit. I won't be long at all.

– Hurry up, mate.

The whole flat is throbbing with the bad atmosphere. His skin prickles with discomfort. Carl feels time turning back on itself in the midday quiet. Reality folding into different shapes. The room gets smaller and closes in on him. He puts the listening device on a shelf at the back. A phone rings somewhere in the block, shattering the silence. Another flat, maybe above, or two doors down.

– Is it my phone?

– Na.

– Is it my phone?

– It's next door, mate.

– Is it my phone?

– You ain't gotta phone, Lloyd.

Lloyd comes running into the living room hobbled by his jeans and underwear round his ankles, his cock flapping about. He looks terrified as he opens a cupboard and empties the jumbled contents onto the floor in a panic. Carl fears he'll look elsewhere and discover the bug.

– Is it my phone?

He pulls out an old house phone with the lead cut off and puts the receiver to his ear.

– Is it my phone?

They can hear the ringing continue in the distance as they stare at each other, and Lloyd puts the phone down and goes back to the toilet. The sound of the flush followed by water running from a tap against the ongoing ring of a distant phone. Lloyd comes back with a handful of cash and they start counting. The phone stops ringing, then starts again.

•

THE SUN IS SHINING AS CARL WALKS BACK TO HIS VAN. BIRDS CALLING against traffic noise. Scream of a gull, rattle of magpie. Carl looks out across the rec. Blue sky and white cloud, broken by buildings behind playing fields. The cloud is rolling, spreading out. It turns grey and darkens as it grows. A shadow moves across high-rises, houses, roads and rec. Everything fades in its path. Desolate dereliction in a dusty nowhere. The buildings look old and haunted against melancholy sky. The rec bare and hard, the earth cracked. The concrete is flaking. It all looks lost, abandoned. Like no one has been there for a century or more. Carl turns and gets in the van, starts it and drives away. Everything is set against him. How can you win when your eyes are sensitive to the light, but you're afraid of the shadows?

Putting a couple of pints of lager down, Carl sits at a table with Mick. In a dark, quiet corner of an old traditional English pub, two men playing darts behind them.

– Cheers. Hear about Lloyd?

– No.

– Terrible. What a way to go.

– What, the heart removed?

– Yeah. Nightmare.

– Yeah.

– What you got for me?

– Nothing, Mick.

– Wad'ya mean, nothing? What you been doin'?

– I've been listening to everyone. They don't know shit. Nobody knows anything.

– You ain't bugged everyone.

– Na. I ain't bugged you.

– Don't get clever, boy. It's me's payin' ya. I wouldn't pay you if I knew it was me, would I?

– Na, but I ain't bugged none'a your lot, 'ave I? D'ya want me to?

– Yeah, fuck it. Why not? Frank and Tom know, so that'll be tricky.

– I can give a couple of bugs to you to hide.

– Yeah, do that.

– It ain't my fault, Mick. Seems nobody knows, or they ain't sayin'.

– Na. Don't worry, something'a come up sooner or later. Long as you're trying, you got no trouble from me. Keep at it.

Carl rubs his chin. He wants Mick to think he might be wasting his money.

– Have you considered that it might not be anyone we know?

– Yeah. But it's all people we do know gettin' it. So, it seems probable it's somebody who has some familiarity, don't ya think?

– Yeah. True. Everyone's getting tugged for questionin'. They had you in yet?

– Yeah. What about you?

– Na, not yet.

Mick leans across the table. His face darkens.

– It's more like serial killer than gangland.

– I thought that 'n all.

– Serial killers usually do women. Sometimes children or queers. But not hard men like us.

– Yeah. So, do you want me to keep listenin'?

– Keep it up for now. We see 'ow it goes. Here, fancy a game a darts?

– I ain't played for years.

– Neither 'ave I. I feel like a game'a darts. If they don't get off that dartboard now, I'm gonna throw a dart in the back of his fuckin' head.

The two men playing leave the darts in the board and walk off, avoiding eye contact. Everyone knows who Mick is round here. Carl feels ashamed. He doesn't like unnecessary intimidation. He never liked bullies.

ANNA LOOKS CARL IN THE EYE. SHE HOLDS HIS FACE CLOSE TO HERS and he feels her look inside, searching. Scanning his mind. He wishes he had sunglasses on.

– What are you hiding?

– Nothing.

– Yes you are. You think you can fool me?

– No.

– It doesn't matter. You don't owe me the truth. If I find something I don't like, I can go.

– Why d'ya keep askin' then? You're gettin' on me fuckin' nerves.

– Do you love me?

– Come on, girl. You know I can't get into all that. It's not healthy.

– I know you. I know what you don't want. I think you're scared of love. But I think you do love me.

– Leave it out.

– What did you think when we first met?

– Same as every girl I meet. I pictured you havin' a wank.

– Dirty bastard. What do you picture when you meet men then?

– I wonder how long it would take for the flesh to come away from the skull if you boiled their head. It's how I gauge 'em. Their strength, or weakness.

– I'd keep that to yourself.

– I will, thanks. Do you want to go for a walk?

– Yeah.

•

Arm in arm along the path in the park, a cool breeze plays with the trees and the bough bows and branches reach and creak as they sway. The magpie calls out a rattle-clacker call and a gold disc in the sky sits near the horizon, above a row of houses. The young mother with her son are there in the same place. She looks pretty, summer dress in the golden light. She looks up and her eyes are empty. She has no soul. The shadow has taken away whatever was there and the look is a hollow look of knowing judgement. The boy playing looks up with the same empty eyes and Carl knows the shadow has caught him too and there's no going back, they're lost forever. Carl sees his long shadow sweep across the ground as they turn on the path, and it's on him and Anna too. A heavy weight drops inside him.

– Let's go back.

– We've only just got here.

– I know, but I wanna go back. D'you mind?

– No. I only come round for a fuck and you getting all romantic with your walks 'n all. I told ya you're in love, ya poof.

– Yeah alright.

•

Back at the flat, Anna smoking and Carl pissing. A bare bulb flickers and fizzes above. The piss slows to a dribble and echoes in the small room, then stops, and Carl sees a reflection of himself as an old man in the yellow water. Hideous mask of exhaustion and pain. No hope in surrender of life. He shudders and a dread creeps through him as he senses a presence behind him. He turns and nobody's there, but the light fizzes and dims and the halo glow around the door looks frightening, as though when he opens it, there will be a different room from the one he came in from. The light dies as he opens the door and Carl's surprised to see the same hallway he'd been in before.

In the living room, Anna is standing with the works held out. Used syringe, blackened spoon. She looks like she's been crying. His blood solidifies in his veins.

– You lied.

– It was one time.

– No. It was more. I told you, I'm not hanging around for this.

– I'm sorry.

– Why are you saying sorry to me? You should be sorry for yourself.

– I dunno what I'm doin'.

– Shut up and fuck me. I'm not coming back again. You'd better make the most of it.

Carl pushes her and she falls back on the sofa. He pulls her skirt up, she lifts her legs and he roughly yanks her knickers off. Smell of sex, hands full of soft girl-flesh. He pushes her arms above her head and she lets him hold them there with one hand, while he undoes his fly. He fucks her like he's punching an enemy he's beaten to the floor.

DESOLATION OF A SLEEPLESS NIGHT. TERRIFIED OF THE NEXT DAY. DRAWN out, doomed and unbearable to get through another afternoon. To make it back to the sad long night. Fear of small, mundane tasks, each becoming monumental, impossible. Overwhelming. Monsters of the everyday. And the breathing, difficult. The air solid, as his lungs ache in frustration at opening and closing, but suffocating somehow. Filled with shadow, spreading within. Invaded by darkness. Hopeless visions of a hanged man. And the fear growing, of the next day and the next night and the never-ending pain of existence and having to survive, to keep going. Again and again. Longing for escape. An end to the racing thoughts. For sweet relief. For peace.

•

Startled at the road vanishing beneath him and the wheel in his hands, Carl jumps in his seat and slows the van down. It's as if he's appeared in his body from nowhere and it's driving, a frightening surprise. He can't recall the moments before and has no idea where he is, or where he's going. How did he get here? Looking at the road winding before him, a country lane, with trees either side, branches reaching and meeting overhead, he feels like he's in a dream. Like a mystic green dream tunnel, twisting and turning with the view tapering to a distant point round the bend, out of sight. Trying to remember where he's going, Carl is lost. Home. He must be going home. But where is he? Bit by bit, he tries to reconstruct the memory of the day in his mind, filling the blanks. Not quite sure if he's making it all up. At work, two jobs in different areas and a break between. Bits of it missing, the order of events distorted somehow. It all seems like a strange hallucination. Nothing is real.

He remembers turning up at the first job early, about half seven, and waiting outside 'til the builder got there. Remembers finishing a fitted bookshelf in a study. The builder had been upset when Carl told him of a dream he'd had the night before. Little sleep, like most nights lately. The fear consuming him, soaked in sweat. And the dream, so vivid and real.

He'd been lying on a bed, naked. Anna was standing at the foot of the bed wearing only a pair of knickers, smiling, and Glen, the builder he was working with, was standing next to the bed, fully clothed and grinning like an idiot. Show him, Carl had said to Anna, and she pulled her underwear down a bit at the front to show Glen a nice, heavy-looking cock, where no bulge had shown in the knickers before. Glen laughed and pointed out that her cock was bigger than Carl's.

I'm not having that, Carl had said, and claimed it was only because he was lying down. Well, go on then. Stand up and show us, Glen had said. Carl stood up and looked down to see his willy looking bigger, more impressive. Not bad, Glen said, chuckling, as he got down on his knees. He licked at the head and got his mouth round it, sucking and slurping between laughter. Anna, nude now, no longer had a cock and her sex was a bald slit. She squealed and giggled, clapping excitedly, as Glen gobbled enthusiastically on Carl's stiff prick. Carl was, on the whole, a lot happier with the scene at that point. It seemed somehow more acceptable.

Glen was disgusted and strangely embarrassed at hearing Carl's dream and couldn't believe Carl had told him. Ashamed almost, that the dream-him had behaved like that. He was quite upset and couldn't look Carl in the eye.

– There's something wrong with you. You ain't right in the head, mate. Why are you dreaming about me suckin' you off?

– I dunno. I didn't do it on purpose, did I? It's a dream, ain't it? They make 'emselves up as they go. Funny though, ain't it?

– No. It's not funny. It's fuckin' weird is what it is.

There was an awkward silence between the two men for a while after. Carl smiled to himself, thinking of how strange people are, with their taboos and culture of conformity. Fragile self-image. The shelving had all been pre-cut to size, so putting it all together was fairly simple. Carl got on with it and finished in time to squeeze in another small job for the afternoon. It was out of town, but he knew it wouldn't take long and the money was worth it. He vaguely remembers the journey to the next job, but it all fades out after that. And here he is, driving along, looking for something familiar to find his way home. The rain comes down heavy. He steers the van through country lanes as the sky darkens and the windscreen wiper buckles on the screen, the view distorted in liquid explosions as he leans over the wheel, squinting, trying to see through the deluge.

Pulling in to the side of the road, to fix the wiper. Carl sits there, watching the rain run down the window and listening to the drum of the downpour on the van roof. Through the storm, he sees a distorted blur of strange shapes through the wet mist and opens the door. Climbing out, the heavy drops hit him in the face and he walks into the grey, into the driving rain, and he's soaked to the bone and his feet drag in wet shoes and his clothes weigh with water and tears mix in the rain on his face and he can't remember and nothing means anything and nothing is real, she's gone and he doesn't know what to do.

JOHN TURNS TO PULL OUT A DRAWER. HARSH LIGHT OF A BARE BULB shining on his bald white head. He brings out a brick of white and puts it on the table. The white brick glows a yellowish phosphor in the sparse, desolate, filthy room.

– Four?

– Yeah.

John reaches in for another white brick and The Hunter brings down the lump hammer head behind his ear. Crack of bone and the big man goes down, smashing his stupid face on the drawer as he drops. The Hunter prepares the unconscious bulk for the sacrifice. Struggling to pull the clothes away, adrenal rush of madness and murder. The nude man moans as a knife slices into his trunk below the ribs. Dark blood spills under stark light glare. Hand in the open body, all the way up to the forearm. Grip on heart, pumping, pumping, pumping. Pulling out the beating muscle into light, and The Hunter bites. Eats the whole thing and the black blood pools around the back of an opened corpse. The Hunter stands, head thrown back in a violent rush as the gold light streams in on a beam from heaven and surges through viscera, like fire in the veins. Ghost with a dog's head, howling. Mad visions of teeth and flesh. God again. The power flowing out to raised hands and up to the head. Nimbus. Golden light fires out through the eyes and mouth and fingertips.

KATE AT THE BAR WITH A GLASS OF WHITE WINE, TALKING TO SOMEONE Carl has never seen.

– Hello, sis, how you doin'?

– Hello darlin'. Sam, this is my brother, Carl. This is Sam from work.

– Alright, Sam?

Carl doesn't want to meet anyone new. He has nothing to say to Sam. He looks away, uninterested. Then looks back and glares into the poor fella's eyes. The man bristles at Carl's bad atmosphere, stare of menace, and he wants to move away.

– Nice to meet you. I'll let you two get on with it. See you soon, Kate.

– Bye, Sam.

– Who's that prick?

– Don't be mean. He's just someone I work with.

The barman raises his eyebrows at Carl.

– I'll 'ave a Hop House. What d'you want?

– I'll have another white wine, please.

The barman pours the drinks and Carl pays.

– Let's sit over there.

They take their drinks to a table in a quiet corner.

– So, how've you been? You don't look well, Carl. Are you takin' care of yourself?

– Yeah, you know. Alright. How about you?

– Just so sad. I can't stop thinking about Dean.

– Me 'n all. Just don't seem real. One moment of madness and there's nothing you can do to change it. Nothin'.

Kate has welled up and Carl looks away.

– I miss his smile.

– Yeah. Fuckin' idiot.

– How 'ave you been coping? People are worried about you.

– Why?

– I got a call from Anna. She said you were acting strange.

– Oh yeah?

– Have you been using?

– No.

– Carl, don't go back.

Carl looks round the pub. People drinking. They're watching him. Pretending to mind their own business. Fear explodes in his gut. They're all robotic. Android spies. He knocks back his pint. Someone laughs and the laugh echoes in his head.

– Are they laughin' at me?

– No, don't be stupid. You're paranoid.

– Ever get the feelin' this nothin' reality has changed?

– What do you mean?

– This don't look like a real pub. It's more like a dream. A film set. A set-up. Upside down. Downward spiral. I gotta go.

– Carl?

– Sorry, sis.

Carl gets up to leave and an android turns away from the bar as he passes. The two men bump into each other and beer spills. The android speaks.

– Watch where you're goin'.

Carl punches the robot in the nose and the angry blood flows in his veins with a mad rush. He lands several more digs in a bloody face, as the man slumps against the bar and the drinks are dropped and Carl walks out into the strange dream-night and Kate follows.

– Carl. Carl.

She stands in the doorway watching him walk away, looks back into the pub at the broken man on the floor with the barman helping him up and starts off after her brother.

Carl looks up to the stars, sharp in a clear black sky, and the moon looks back like an all-seeing eye. Something moves in a tree and Carl stops. It's a bird, unlike any Carl has ever seen. He stares for a moment, vaguely aware that he's never seen a bird in the night before. The ghost-bird watches Carl with fixed eyes and he is mesmerised. As he looks at it, the bird becomes part of the tree and is no longer there. Carl turns and walks on.

Kate catches up with him and Carl swings round as he hears her approach.

– Carl. What's wrong?

– I'm alright.

– Why did you do that?

– What?

– Why did you hit him?

– Something weren't right in there. It was all set up against me.

– It wasn't. Carl, there was nothing going on.

– He knocked into me on purpose, to stop me leaving.

Kate looks at Carl's face. His eyes are distant. He looks alarmed.

– Nothin' was happening, Carl. You need help.

– Why don't you fuck off? For all I know, you're part of it.

– What are you on about?

– You invited me there.

– Carl, you need help.

– Leave me alone.

Carl turns and walks way.

– Just leave me alone.

A LONELY ROOM. BARE BULB ALIGHT IN THE GLOOM. SOFT FUZZ OF blurred focus and faraway feeling of seeing himself as another person, watching the other him, there on the sofa. Drifting through distorted time of no meaning and strange understanding of how funny it all is. The pain. The desolation, the lost hope and fear of everything. Carl knows it in his heart. None of this is real. Being alone for so long, as the terrible days go by, drifting into day after night after day, is better than the cold loneliness of being around other people. No connection to anyone, or anything. Remote, detached. Removed. Nowhere. A ghost in the void. Drifting.

Recordings of voices, meaningless conversations drift through his mind. Echo and loop in and out of the space around him. Staring through a wall, into nothing. Carl's attention is sucked into the television, the horror of the blank screen and the realisation that it's watching him. He feels its presence in the room, rude intrusion of being observed. Invasion of mind, he knows it can hear his thoughts too. Exposed. He turns it on for dull distraction. Daytime drivel.

What a load of shit. Who watches this?

The sound of a lorry reversing outside is disturbing. The *beep beep beep* of reverse warning with engine rattle and hiss of brakes, as the vehicle parks and the workmen's voices are echoing in Carl's head and he feels like they're doing something to him. Setting it all up to fuck him over somehow. The TV is invading his mind, an irritation deep inside. Planting a coded message of some sort, ready to activate at a later time. A programme of meaningless nonsense and the voices are mixing with the workmen's noise outside in a conspiracy of unbearable sound to confuse and torture him. The lorry and the workmen are somehow connected. Carl switches the TV off, but it's still there, an ominous presence in the corner. Every cell in his body is vibrating. Nothing makes any sense. Uncomfortable fear of something terrible about to happen.

Looking at the skin moving across his hands, Carl has an alarming sense of someone else being in the room with him. He's not alone. Looking round the room, he sees nobody. But someone is there. He understands, with a lurching drop of his soul, as the room distorts around him, that the spectre is in him.

As his heart twists, he wonders if he's driving, or just a passenger. It occurs to him that he may be the invasion and this body is not his. He tries to think back, all the memories. Do they belong to him, or did he acquire them when he moved in? No, he decides, I'm me. This is my body and something else has invaded it. He wants it to leave, but how long has it been there, and where does it end and he begin?

•

Ringtone shatter of peace in the mind and startled horror of someone calling. Mick. Carl eyes the phone with dread and a cold stone in his gut. He lets it ring out. It starts again. He wishes he could ignore it.

– Hello, Mick.

– What's happening, Carl?

– Nothing much. How ya doin'?

– I'm wonderin' what I'm payin' you for. Where you been?

– I ain't been out much, mate. Ain't seen no one.

There's a lot of recordings to get through 'ere. I gotta keep on top of it, Mick, or we might miss somethin'. You want me to keep goin'?

– Alright. Just checkin'. Yeah. Keep it up. Let me know if you pick up on anythin', woncha?

– Yeah, mate. Will do.

– See ya later.

– Yeah, see ya later.

Carl hangs up, then throws the phone across the room.

– Fuck off.

DISTURBANCE IN A DARK CORNER. THREE BIG MEN ARE BEATING another man. The smaller man is struck with a heavy blow. He goes down with more fists landing as he folds and collapses. Carl watches as the three thugs kick and stamp down the man on the floor. He hides behind the pillar of an arch, keeping as still as he can. He knows if they see him, he could be next. The battered man is trying to shield himself. A sickening *crack* as he's kicked in the side and he throws his head back in pain. For a moment, his twisted face is dimly lit by a distant street lamp. Carl feels a sensation like a punch to the gut as he sees the face. It's his own. The man they are beating is him. He walks away, fast strides, then staggering, stumbling disorientation as he tries to comprehend what he's just seen.

Along a dark street, Carl sees a shadow man disappear into darkness. Wind sends dust and debris down the narrow road. The shops are closed, and the windows are black in the flats above. In an open window, vertical blinds blow gently. The darkness behind them gives Carl an empty sense that something is about to destroy him. He stares up at it as he passes below. A row of arches ahead, where the shadow man hid. Each arch a lurid mystery of horrible possibility. Carl passes the first and second archways. Cold fear in the abyss of each. At the third, a fist launches from the shadows and catches Carl in the side of his face. He recovers to find himself dragged into the darkness. As punches land from all directions, he tries to fight back, but it's no good. The men are huge. He has a vague feeling of inevitability as he falls to the floor and feet stomp down on him. He has already seen this and knows what happens.

Aware of the cold air on his skin, Carl looks through the black space around him and groans. Pain throbs in every part of him. As his eyes grow used to the dark, he sees he is in a room. He feels chains round his wrists and ankles and realises he is naked. In the corner, a shadow man sits facing him, only partly revealed in the darkness. Carl moves his head to the faint light behind him and an ache tears through his neck and head. Above him, a sliding window, slightly open, with vertical blinds swaying in a breeze.

Light flashes across the window and for a moment, the shadow face is lit. A frightening mask, hideous and beautiful. It's Anna's face, a vicious smirk.

– Anna. Anna, what's goin' on?

The shadow is silent. Carl strains his eyes through darkness to see the face again, but it's different now. It looks like him. It's his face on the mask and it's grinning at him, menacing, leering at his nudity. He tries to hide from that terrible grin, but the chains hold him exposed.

•

Door entry buzz, sound-jar of angry nerves, irritation to the core. Unwanted interruption of sitting alone with the curtains drawn, full light of the day refused entry. Only thin rays light the dust that dances in a lonely room. The outside another world.

What now?

Carl lifts the receiver with reluctant acceptance of whatever comes his way. No point resisting the inevitable.

– Hello?

– It's me.

Anna. Carl is relieved, but also unsure. Anna doesn't fit in this picture now. He wants her back, but she has moved so far from his reach. He is detached. Removed from contact with these humans. These strange animals. His flesh is no longer his own. How can he share it with anyone else? He hears her footsteps echo in the stairwell and quietly shuts the door. Looking through the spyhole, he sees her walking towards him. Skirt, heels, tight top and long hair. Her face is hidden in shadow. The half-lit image of silhouette Anna in a dream corridor, through distorted lens, is a shadow girl. Ghost girl in a haunted hallway. The vision repeats in his mind as he opens the door slightly. He stands there staring at her, shocked expression in his faraway eyes. He doesn't speak, doesn't know what to say. He feels his image shudder and distort before her. Anna fades to nothing, leaving her eyes hanging in the air, then returns, solid. Carl flips a switch in his mind and a golden force field ignites around him.

– Hello. Aren't you gonna let me in?

Carl opens the door wide and steps to one side, gesturing for Anna to enter.

– You not talking to me?

– No. I mean, yeah. I am.

Anna laughs.

– What's got into you? Why you acting like a freak?

– Dunno. Weren't expectin' ya. You didn't ring me.

– It's a surprise.

He thinks she might be mocking him.

– I was just coming this way and wanted to make sure you're okay. How are you?

– Yeah, I'm alright.

Carl studies Anna in the dim light. It looks like her, but something is different. He can't be sure it's the same Anna he knew. Suspicion tears through him. He holds it down, trying not to let it show in his face. Who is this being? She looks at him sharply. She heard his thought. He must think quietly. The air is strange around him and his movements feel awkward and forced. She glides across the room, fluid, and sits down smiling at him. The smile changes. Red lipstick grin of sinister knowing. What does she know? Penetration of searching eyes. Mesmerised, he holds her stare. Her movements are slow, hypnotic. Carl, held in a trance, wants her to undress, to put on a show.

He feels power surge through his veins as he understands her as prey. She has come to give herself. But it's a trick. A lure. An illusion. She is a hypnotic predator, who could strike with unseen speed at any moment. The power stutters in Carl's heart. Images move in the wall behind her. A face, screaming agony breaks free from the shadows. It's a sign to Carl. Something is wrong. He's torn. Conflict, confusion. Should he pull her clothes off and fuck her, or throw her out? He punches Anna in the face, grabs her by the hair and bites into her cheek, blood running down his chin. She sits there smiling serenely.

– Why are you staring at me? Put the kettle on.

Carl is pulled out of his trance and goes to the kitchen. He fills the kettle, the sound of running water echoes in the void. Anna is talking, but the sound of the water heating to boil is mixing with the words and he can't hold on to what she says. The kettle noise is coming from her mouth.

The thin beam of light through a crack in the curtains stops. The lit dust disappears. A shadow moves across

Anna's face and spreads through the room. A chill runs through Carl, as her serene smile again becomes a leering grin. The boiling water and steam from the kettle are loud and as he reaches for a mug, it falls and shatters on the worktop. Instead of clearing up the broken pieces, Carl gets another mug and prepares the tea. The boiling noise goes on forever. Carl looks at Anna. Her lips are moving, but all he hears is boiling water. He turns it off at the switch.

– Have you come back?

– No, Carl. I can't see you like that. Not how it was.

– Why?

– Because you weren't straight with me. Remember how messy it was last time? Remember, before you got well?

– I'm alright.

– You're not.

Anna gets up and throws back the curtains. Light pours in, Anna is lit like an angel. A halo round a supernatural being. The light comes from in her, as well as around her. Of darkness and light. All-powerful, standing before him, in his living room, looking at his pitiful existence. He feels himself shrinking in her presence.

– Why're you sitting around in the dark? Look at this place. It's a fucking tip in here. Looks like you've been burgled.

Carl shrugs. He scans the room and vaguely thinks he probably ought to clear it up at some point. The room is like one he knows.

– You look good.

– Thanks.

– Wanna fuck?

– No, Carl.

– Yeah you do. Why would you come here? You only come when you want sex.

– I just want to know you're alright. See if you needed anything.

– I need to fuck.

– It's not happening.

– I'm sorry about what happened. It was a moment of weakness. I shouldn't have hid it from ya.

– You should look after yourself. That's what matters, Carl.

– I ain't done it since.

– Well, that's for you to know. I can't help you with that.

– I'm alright now.

– I don't think you are, Carl. You won't get help either.

Carl steps closer to Anna. He looks into her eyes. This isn't Anna. This entity is here on a snide mission. What does it want? Smells good though. He wants to keep it here and possess it physically, but he wants it to leave him alone too. As he stares into its eyes, the pupils dilate. They grow larger until the eyes are completely black. He is sucked in. The blackness swallows him.

– Why don't you fuck off?

– Alright Carl. I'll go if you want.

She turns to the door and Carl puts his hand on her arm.

– No, wait.

– What?

Carl leans in and kisses Anna, taking her by surprise. Anna responds and they stand there lost in the kiss. Anna breaks away.

– I've gotta go, Carl.

– I don't know if I want you to stay or go.

– I know. You need a bath. Sort yourself out.

She walks out without looking back.

CARL STOPS A RECORDING, REWINDS AND PLAYS IT BACK. THERE IT IS. An address. A holding house. Full of it. Full of what? Something valuable. Arrived yesterday and stored there for a while. Carl smiles. Easy to listen in and find out comings and goings. Easy to wait for the right moment.

Sitting outside in the van, parked up the road a bit, Carl watches and listens. He's put a device near the door too. Tom and Frank walk out, talking. They get into a car and pull away. Carl waits a few minutes, then gets out of the van. He opens the side door and pulls out a lever and a screwdriver.

At the back of the house, French doors, double-glazed. Cheap shit. Nobody realises how easy it is to get those open. Carl puts the screwdriver between the doors, where the latch is, and prises them apart. He puts the crowbar in the gap and levers the latch out of the catch and pulls the doors open. No sweat.

In a room, parcels piled high. Must be fifty boxes in there. Carl grabs a few and puts them in a sports bag. He goes out the back and levers the doors back together. Back in the van, he's sweating, but he's done it. He starts the engine and pulls away. As he passes the stash-house, he sees a shadow fall across the windows and door.

THE HUNTER BRINGS A CLAW HAMMER DOWN ON THE BACK OF A BIG, square head, white light flash in the eyes. Man goes down hard, face bounce on the floor. Clothes stripped off. Naked body of fallen thug, prone. Cut under the cage. Hand right in, up to the elbow, grabs beating ticker and pulls down and out and free. Blood flows and grows a dark puddle, as The Hunter bites into the pumping heart. Swallow and bite, swallow and bite, 'til it's all gone and the magic flows and rushes in the veins like crazy. Power grows in ecstatic bursts of building ecstasy and transforms The Hunter into a superbeing. Mad god with a vulture's head. Black eyes in a fixed stare, portals to nowhere. The whole room lights up and shines like heaven.

– 'ALLO MICK.

– Another one got done last night.

– Yeah, I 'eard.

– One of ours.

– Who was it?

– Jason.

– Fuckin' 'ell. Same way?

– Yeah, I think so.

– Who the fuck's done that? Jason'd never let someone get the better of 'im.

– One'a the 'ardest cunts I've ever known.

– Yeah.

– I heard you've been out and about again.

– Yeah, well. Been busy. I got a tug from Old Bill, didn't I. I want to know as much as you do, now.

– What did they say?

– Ah, ya know. Same old shit. What d'ya know, who d'ya know, where were ya. Who've you seen lately. All that.

– Did they lean on ya heavy?

– A bit. They found me prints at some of 'em.

– Oh yeah?

– I told 'em, I said, course ya did. I been round there ain't I? I know 'em.

– What did they say?

– Not a lot. They asked me if I been up to no good. I told 'em to fuck off. No charge anyway. They let me go in the end.

– I'm getting nervous, Carl. We had a good thing runnin' 'ere. Everyone under manners. Now, they're all eyein' each other up. This is fucked.

– I did catch somethin' of interest to ya, Mick.

– Oh yeah?

– You got a couple'a your boys on the take.

– No fuckin' way.

– Yeah.

– Who?

– Tom an' Frank.

– Oh you're fuckin' jokin'?

– I ain't, mate. They're at it. Have a listen if ya want, but in the meantime, get someone to 'ave a count up. I ain't messin' with ya, Mick. I 'eard 'em talkin'.

WALKING ACROSS THE AFTERNOON PARK. CARL SEES THE SAME woman on the bench, watching her boy playing. She looks up and catches his eye. He holds the look and she smiles. He smiles back. Carl changes direction and walks towards them. As he gets closer, he sees the woman is Anna. He stops. He looks at the boy and the boy is him. Carl as a toddler. Exactly the same as his mother's pictures of him. The boy stops playing and looks back at Carl and they're both staring at him. Little Carl and Anna. He walks again and as he nears them, they change. They're not him or Anna. They're the same boy and woman he'd seen before. Dark clouds billow above and a shadow moves over the park. The woman stands up and holds the little boy's hand as he approaches. The shade falls across them. The boy fades and vanishes to nothing. The sun reappears and Carl finds himself holding her hand where the little boy was and they walk away together.

GIRL, TIED LIKE A SACRIFICE. NAKED. EXPOSED. HANDS ABOVE HER head. Whip, snap of leather strap, maniac grin on a clown face. Idiot mask. Scruffy clothes, like a tramp. Her dancing to a slow-slap rhythm of the sting. Shadows grow in the grim corners of the room, her clothes crumpled on the floor. The filth and decay, the desolation and the bad dreams of a nowhere ghost. And every red stripe across bare girl flesh keeps the darkness from creeping up on him. Raw and ready in transcendence, to transform them into supernatural beings in dramas of played out power in love and lust with no lies. Exquisite agony of ecstasy, pleasure in pain. And he sees it and the fire in his blood burns. Mysterious diabolism in exorcism of madness in a dim mist.

Until the shadows retreat and wait in corners, 'til next time. The night keeps creeping up when it thinks he's not looking. Visions in the walls around them form and morph. Shapes appearing and disappearing, recognised as terrible beings through fearful eyes. The shadows watch, as the whipping stops. Strap dropped. Rough hands on soft skin, squeeze and grope. Stroke wet heat and they melt together, become a part of the writhing shapes in the walls and the space between them.

Tom and Frank pull off the main road. They've been driving for a long time. Down another country lane and the road narrows off. Going to pick up some dough for Mick. Farm boys, apparently. They don't know this lot. Some new fellas Mick's got running out in the sticks.

– I think it's just up 'ere.

– Looks like an entrance to a field.

– Yeah, pull in 'ere, Tom. This is it.

They stop the motor and Frank jumps out, opens a heavy cattle gate. He gets back in and they drive on into a narrow, grassy lane.

– He said park up outta sight and they'll come an' find us.

– I'm gonna pull up. This'll do.

The two men sit and wait. They've got about twenty minutes before the others show up, Mick told them to get there early.

– Why did he want us to get 'ere before 'em? We usually let 'em wait for *us*.

– Dunno. I'm not sure who this lot are. Or what the paperwork's for.

– How much is it?

– Fuck knows, Frank. I dunno.

– Seems a bit weird to me, all this. Somethin' ain't right.

– Yeah. I had a funny feelin' all day, but if Mick says it's alright, it's alright.

– Yeah. Maybe this lot work for someone important, or somethin'.

– Mick might be doin' work for them, for all I know. This could be a pay-off. Fuck knows.

Tom's head opens up in two places, as the screen and quarter-light shatter. Tiny glass fragments glitter like jewels.

Claret and brain all over Frank. A rushing sound in his ears, he opens the door as his shoulder explodes and he falls trying to get out of the car. He feels his face collapse, cheek bone splinters, and spluttering through blood in broken jaw, as he lies there looking up and it all goes numb as the shrill tone of the wind in his ears turns to singing and the lights dance and the silhouette figures looking down on him grow and blur into blackness.

ALONE IN A SAD STREET. THE HOUSES ALL LOOK EMPTY. GREY SKY. Unsolid sun, seen through spectral clouds, moving in the poison air. All below in shade. Parked cars abandoned, old, with kicked-off wing mirrors and cracked screens. Windows knocked through. Flat tyres. Decay. Rust. Sealer bags and empty cans in the gutter. Dog shit on the path. Old mattresses and broken-down furniture in front yards.

Carl walks, hands in pockets, collar turned up to the dirty breeze. Wonders why he is there. He's looking for an answer, but can't remember what the question is. He thinks it might be something important, so he keeps walking, scraping the soles of his shoes on the paving stones. A nowhere shuffle, careless of destination and no hurry.

Where is everyone? It's as though all the people were wiped out. Disease, war, or some unknown disaster that missed him somehow. Desolation of lonely road. It occurs to him that this is what peace is. He stops and looks around. No sound but the slow wind. Something moves at the side of his eye. A shadow man. The dark figure hides round the corner of a high wall. He turns back and the sight of a house on the corner makes his gut drop in a cold terror. He stands mesmerised by the small house, torn between revulsion and a compulsion to go inside.

Round the back, a door, peeled paint in a rotten frame. He pulls the handle and it breaks off in his hand, but the door moves in the soft rot. He kicks it and it swings open. Inside, damp smell, floorboards missing, and plaster fallen from walls. Laths showing and brick. Torn wallpaper with black mould. Broken windows. The kitchen is derelict, filth piled up in the sink. No furniture in the front room.

The stairs creak and risers and steps are gone here and there. The runner is cracked. The whole thing looks like it'll collapse. Upstairs, the landing wall is crumbling, old graffiti, layers of paint. The bathroom is cold. Smashed toilet, shit on the floor. Bath full of mould and dirt. Carl gags and walks to a bedroom.

As he goes in, he stops, frozen. A hanged man swings gently in the corner of the room. Kicked-over stool below. A shadow hand grips his heart and the world falls away beneath him. The body turns slow and he sees the face. It's his face. Stretched neck, distorted features, but it's him. He watches himself hang there for a moment, then backs out of the room and closes the door.

Outside, a bird flies in a dark sky with a bright white sun. Black cloud billows. A storm bursts in the green air and the bird falls apart. Disintegrates in a blizzard of buzzard feathers and fuzz. Wings falling. It all comes tumbling down in the wind and the rain. Carl watches it drop, spiralling down, broken bird. He feels himself falling too, as a shadow spreads along the street and moves across him.

He walks over to where the bird hits the ground. Standing over it, looking down, he sees it's still alive. The smashed bird moves its head and looks him in the eye. The beak opens and a strangled, high-pitched noise comes out, but he hears the message projected into his head by some telepathic trick.

– You can't escape.

Carl recoils, stamps on the bird's head to silence the transmission. The beak and fragile bones crunch under his shoe. But it's Anna's face his foot is on and she's lying naked in the rain, bloody and bruised. Her mutilated body bleeding and the blood mixing with the raindrops and running away to the gutter. He lifts his foot to see her face half caved-in and stumbles back, falling on the kerb. Sitting in a dirty puddle, soaked to the bone, Carl stares at the nude girl in disbelief. He gets up and walks away, looking around to see if anyone saw. Nobody about. He looks back at the body, naked on the pavement. A magpie lands next to her and pecks at the broken face.

Delirium hits him in a spinning rush. Brain floats off in a lurid liquid. Confused, disoriented, staggering. The street scene softens and blurs, shuddering and stuttering like a video glitch. Everything shifts this way, then that, like a ship on high waves in a rough sea. He falls on his hands and knees, scrambling about in the wet, oily rainbow patterns on the path, and he's broken and beaten and he doesn't know why. Can't remember what happened. He looks back along the pavement. He can't see Anna. He can't see anything through the grey haze of the rain. He gives up and lies there on the cold, wet concrete, shivering.

– Hello Mick.

– Alright, mate.

– You 'eard about Tom an' Frank?

– Yeah. Shame, ain't it? Lovely boys. Known 'em all me life.

– Yeah. You see one'a the Turks got done 'n all? Same way as the others.

– Yeah. They've gone 'n shot up a couple'a Kurds for it.

– Did they? I ain't seen the news. They're always shootin' each other anyway.

– Yeah. You been buggin' that lot?

– Some of 'em. But they always want to meet up in a motor.

– What about the Ians?

– Russians 'n Romanians?

– Yeah.

– Some of 'em. Hard to get into, that lot. Don't really go into their houses. A few of theirs got done 'n all.

– I heard it was them doin' it.

– What, the Russians?

– Yeah.

– There's been a few shootin's 'n all with them lot. I reckon it's gonna kick off, mate.

– Everyone's getting spooked. Old Bill ain't got nothin'.

– D'ya want me to keep goin'?

– Might as well. Never know what'll turn up.

– Alright, mate.

– See ya later.

– Yeah. See ya later.

Carl puts the phone down and turns the engine over. He swings the van round and drives into the estate. All quiet. Several youths standing around at the back of the car park.

Hoods up. Carl pulls up at the back corner, where he can see the whole estate. Nobody else about.

Where are these cunts?

He thinks about leaving, but can't be bothered to rearrange and decides to wait a moment. He leaves the motor running.

Movement in the wing mirror catches his eye and he presses the lock button. The door latches click. Two men either side, pointing handguns.

– Open the fuckin' door.

It's a set-up. Carl considers not opening the door. He weighs up quickly in his mind how long it would take to release the handbrake, chuck it in gear and drive off. Guns look like semis. Are they loaded? Probably. How many shots could these pricks fire off before he got away? Probably couldn't hit a beer can at ten paces, but he's point blank.

Carl presses the button and the locks click again. Man on the passenger side opens the door, reaches in and grabs the bag on the bench seat. He looks inside. It's the tackle from Mick's place.

You're messing with the wrong people.

– Shut ya noise.

The man has his hood up and a scarf pulled up over his nose. Something familiar about him. Carl thinks he might be involved with the fella from Clarence's place. The one he gave a kicking to outside John's flats. The man on the driver's side opens the door.

– Give me the keys.

– Ya got the gear, now fuck off.

The man at his side goes for the ignition and Carl grabs the gun hand, trapping it in his lap. There's a struggle. As the man lands two punches on the side of Carl's head, Carl manages to hit him in the face with his elbow and get control of the gun hand. The other man with the bag is pointing the gun at Carl, shouting something. Carl can't hear what he's saying. He pushes the clutch pedal, throws the stick into reverse and lets off the handbrake. A shot fires off, but Carl can't tell which one of them fired, or if anyone got hit. His ears are ringing. He puts his foot down, catching the man on the passenger side with the open door. It hits him, but not with enough speed to take him out, just knocks him over. Another bang echoes out as the van hits a low wall behind it and Carl jerks back in his seat. He pulls on the gun arm and traps it under his left leg, barring it with his right, then puts the van into first. The man he's got hold of is still punching at him frantically. Carl feels almost nothing as the adrenalin burns through him. Just thuds of dull pain. Force field turned up to ten. He drives forward and hits a parked car, slamming the door on the trapped man, crushing him between vehicles. He lets go of the arm and reverses as he sees the other man getting up and aiming the gun. He smashes straight into him, and then hits the low wall again. He pulls forward a bit and gets out of the van. The man is a mess on the floor, moaning. He picks up the bag, chucks it into the van, slams the door, gets back in, rolls the van over the crushed body in front of him and drives off. Pulling out of the estate, he joins traffic on the main road.

•

   – Everyone thinks you're a cunt.
   – Fuck off.
   – You're weak.
   – Leave me alone.

●

Carl parks down a side road and walks to a petrol station to fill a can. He drives to the edge of town. An old trading estate with an overgrown grassy area at the back, out of sight from the main buildings. He pulls onto the grass. The pistol is down by the handbrake. Carl picks it up, checks the catch, and shoves it into the waistband at the back of his trousers. He grabs the bag with the goods in and chucks it on the grass. Pouring petrol all over the footwell, both sides, under the bonnet, on the floor under the passenger door, some in the tank with the diesel and the rest in the back. He leaves the cap off the diesel and shuts the doors. It's the fumes that do a good job. He waits a while, letting them build up. He needs a couple of rags, so he sacrifices his socks. Hangs a petrol-soaked sock out the passenger door, leaving it slightly ajar. The diesel won't go up like a petrol tank. Not immediately anyway, but it will go. A bit of petrol in there will make fumes. A petrol-soaked sock hanging out of the tank too. He picks up the bag, gets a few steps back, lights a screwed-up piece of paper and chucks it at the petrol puddle below the door and walks away.

Fire sweeps through the van in a moment. Carl doesn't look back. The vehicle is quickly consumed. Flames lick at the sad, grey sky behind him. Eerie sound shadow, spectral movement against the desolate silence and derelict emptiness of broken-down warehouses.

●

In a bar on the other side of town, two buses and a short walk later. Quiet place in the afternoon. Sitting in a booth, with a glass of whisky, he reports the van stolen. Looking around at the dull furnishings and the soft light in a strange calm of no-work drunks. Acceptance of life as it is. No grip. No control. A leaf in the wind, all a dream. He feels the gun and opens the bag, looking at the light brown bricks. He scans the room, nobody watching. Puts the pistol in the bag with the bricks.

He sips his whisky and leans back in the seat. The barmaid is good-looking and her smile is friendly. He could stay here forever, he thinks, with the low lights and quiet atmosphere. No time exists in here. As the warm liquid runs down his gullet, he feels the heat slide and spread through his throat and down into his gut. The peace of the place in the dim light folds in on him, protecting him from the outside. This bar is all there is. Nothing can get to him in here. Nothing else exists. He looks at a man on a stool at the bar. The man looks away. The pretty barmaid is lost in her own thoughts, clearing glasses and wiping a table, and no one is bothering anyone else. If only he could just stay here. He sees out the front, through a window to the street. It's a silent scene of people going about their own business, but it looks like it's playing on a big TV screen. That world has nothing to do with him.

He remembers a time, as a small boy, being in a similar place with his father. He'd been treated differently that day. Not mocked, or scolded, or knocked about. The place was quiet, like this one. The old man had spoken in a low voice to another man at the bar. Almost a whisper, like in a library, or church. And he'd sat there sucking his juice through a straw, swinging his legs under the chair, as he looked round the darkened room, content with this moment. There was something mystical about the scene, the way the sun came into the dim room and lit the bar, like an altar. The barman glowed in the beam, like a saint or a saviour serving sacramental serums to redeem the devoted. He remembered thinking, I'm going to sit in these holy places a lot when I grow up.

IN A CROWDED BAR. ONE OF THE CLUBS ANNA RUNS FOR MICK. MUSIC TOO loud, so you have to shout. Anna looks round the room. She's bored and scans for easy prey. Why not? A trendy place, plastic people. Fake tan, tight shirts, gym muscles. Girls like dolls. Lips, nails, eyelashes, short dresses and heels. Empty. The men too. Like a well-wrapped but dull present. Pretty paper, ribbon and bow, with no decent gift inside. She doesn't feel right. Looking at all the people packed into the long, small room, she feels out of place and misses Carl. As many people as there are in here, she feels as if she's in a vacuum. Detached. Floating. The cramped space around her is at once uncomfortably close, and at the same time infinitely vast. The noise of music and shouting is echoing in her head. Eating into her mind.

Sarah says something in her ear, but she can't hear. She sees her looking at the bar. Anna follows her gaze and a fella on a barstool nods. His smile is confident, but friendly. She smiles back. He'll do. She sips her drink and holds his eyes for a moment, then looks away. Gotcha.

– He looks alright.

– Yeah.

– He's been eyeing you up.

– Has he?

– You want 'im, or what? Cos if not, I will.

– I tell you what. I'll see if I like 'im, if not, he's yours.

Sarah laughs.

– Slut.

– Yeah, so what?

Anna looks back to the bar and catches his eye. Her glassy gaze drops to his crotch. She wets her lips with her tongue. Her eyes slide back up to meet his. He smiles again and she walks over and stands next to him.

– You gonna buy me a drink, or what?

– That's a bit forward. I don't even know your name.

Anna laughs

– Anna.

– Hello Anna. I'm Shane. Nice to meet you.

– Nice to meet you too.

– What you drinking?

– Jack and Coke, please.

He turns to the bar and she empties her glass, side-eying him. Looks good. Well kept. Not posh but pronounces his Ts. She watches him order the drinks. Of course, she could have her drink for free, but she enjoys the game.

– Here you go.

– Thanks.

Distorted funk, scratched up in a hip-hop beat, is filling her head. Anna nods and the bass touches her at a deep level.

– What brings you to this dive?

– The girls. What about you?

– The boys.

He laughs and she smiles.

– Bit of a poser's joint though.

– Yeah. But it's good for an easy pickup.

– Cheeky.

– You started it.

Anna pushes her hair over her ear, puts a foot on the bar rail showing a bit more thigh and downs her drink. She stands there looking hot and watches him drink his, trying to catch up.

– It's too noisy in here. D'you wanna come outside for a smoke?

– I don't smoke, but I'll come with you.

Anna nods to Sarah and Sarah smiles. Outside, the cool air is alive. Everything looks sharp. The moon glows in the black night. Anna lights a cigarette, sucks it and blows out the smoke as she looks at Shane. Shane grins like a Cheshire cat. She takes another pull, then drops it and watches the orange end roll away to the gutter.

– What do you like?

– I like takin' advantage of boys.

She puts her hand on his crotch and feels his cock through his jeans. She leans in and they kiss and she feels it swell behind the rough denim. He puts his hand on her thigh and strokes up under her short skirt. He stops at the top. She breaks the kiss and they smile. He puts his hand between her legs, and she moves her feet apart a bit and he rubs her through her knickers. She looks through him, glass eyes in a fixed stare. Anna kisses him again.

Falling back in a black hole, endless drop of careless kicks and no-hope fear, of lost love and loveless lust. She knows this good clean boy will treat her nice and she can keep him going as long as she likes. Easy. Too easy. Boring dates of empty lies. Probably good for a fuck now and then, but that's all. Maybe not even. Most of these men have got all the chat, but when it comes down to it, they're done in a few minutes and she has to finish herself. She feels a void in her heart. A sinking into dark thick fluid to drown in empty need.

She breaks the kiss.

– I gotta go.

– Why?

– Just do. Gimme your number. I'll call you.

He tries not to show his disappointment, but it's there for her to see in the effort of a blank face. He gives her the number and she pecks him on the cheek. He tries for more, but she's already walking away. Back in the bar, she tells Sarah she's going home.

– I've warmed him up for ya.

– I bet you have. Don't worry, I've got one sorted.

Sarah nods at a man standing next to her. Anna gives him an approving glance and blows a kiss at her friend.

Outside, she rings Carl.

– Hello?

– Yeah.

– What are you doing?

– Nothing.

– See you in about fifteen minutes.

She cuts him off before he can reply.

•

In the morning, strange calm. Anna making breakfast, Carl staring out the window. Thinking about last night, Anna's return to him. Not sure what to make of it. He feels like she's setting him up for the drop. Some betrayal. Nothing makes sense. He didn't complain or question her showing up at some dark hour of the dreamtime. He couldn't sleep anyway. And besides, what man can resist? This divine and spectral creature appearing like a wraith in the horror of another lost night. Short skirt, low-cut top, heels and red lips. She breezed in and took control, as she does. And through the illusion of his command, as he forced her to play such degrading games, he knew all along he was just a tool. A portal for her escape.

He never could resist. She knew it. Now, he wonders what there is between them. He wants to believe it is the old Anna he's always known making breakfast, as though they were a happy couple of lovebirds on a bright day, but he's sure it's not her. No, that Anna is gone. This Anna is an imposter. A succubus to steal his soul, his essence, his thoughts, like the TV, soul-suck vortex, the shadows. Yes, that's it. She has been taken by the shadows. Anna is working as part of a collective attempt to destroy Carl. The shadow people are attacking on all fronts. Through the telly, through Anna, through shadow, through all the people he works with. This is what the killings are. The superbeing that's carrying out the murders is part of it all.

Carl searches for the answer. They're all in on it. Maybe Mick too. There's nothing he can do for now, except survive. Keep going. Play along. Pretend he doesn't know. If he lets on, the game is up. The spell is broken. Perhaps they're just using him for some end he doesn't understand. If they find out he knows, they might end him. Switch him off.

Carl is sitting on the sofa, watching Anna in the kitchen. Succubus. Beautiful monster. At the same time as being terrified of her, his cock is hard in his jeans. Anna making bacon, the smell of it, her in nothing but a T-shirt. He looks at her legs, all the way up to the hem of the T-shirt showing the lower swell of her cheeks, teasing. Showing more every time she bends or reaches. Carl watches, rubbing himself through his jeans. He knows he will take her again after food. Animal need above all else. He understands the game. She is tricking him. A lure. Or perhaps keeping an eye on him. Why else? Carl knows when he takes her, he possesses her. She is lost in lust, an animal on fire. His magic is stronger than hers when he fucks her. Or is it?

He's mesmerised by the swell of her cheeks, drawn in like a magnetic force. Peeping, tantalising, taunting. Nothing else has meaning. He's behind her, lifting the T-shirt, kissing her neck and she turns to him with a bacon sandwich on a plate between them.

– Here you go. Eat this.

– Thanks.

They sit together, eating their breakfast in silence. Hunger and lust for the smell of meat and the taste. They finish the food and look at each other. Anna smiles. Carl reaches for her and she tries to escape, but he's got her pinned down and the T-shirt comes off easy.

•

Anna in the hall, about to leave. Carl hasn't said a word or looked her in the eye for over an hour. They stand there, like statues looking at each other, and time escapes. Everything around Anna dissolves to a blur. Her halo shines in the dim distortion. A strange being. Her eyes alight. The vision swims and shimmers before him.

– Are you alright, Carl?

– Yeah.

– It was nice to see you.

– Yeah.

– I'm gonna go now.

– Are you comin' back?

– Let's see how it goes.

– Yeah.

The image shudders and distorts. Halo flickers, grows and shrinks. Grows again. Carl stands, swaying. The light in her eyes is like the sun. Anna fades to nothing, except the bright points where her eyes are. Carl hears the door slam shut and time returns. Standing in the hallway by himself, Carl has no idea if she was ever there.

●

Dim light through sliding window, vertical blinds on a dark room. Chained down, wrists and ankles spread wide. Cool air from the open window blows across his naked skin. Carl feels his exposure through the pain of his broken, battered body. The shadow man watches his discomfort. Carl can't see his face, but knows it is grinning. Time stops and the long wait for inevitable doom drags on and on.

The shadow man stands and walks to where Carl lies. He kneels next to him and gently runs cold fingers over his chest and abdomen. Unwanted sensual touch, like a lover teasing, but the tease is a taunt of something terrible to come. Anna standing behind the shadow slightly to his left, lit by a light that falls nowhere else. A shining apparition in the dark. As though the light is emitting from inside of her. Her face a leering smirk. She enjoys his agony. She thrives on his degradation and fear. Her face has a look of excitement, as though aroused by what she sees. Ecstatic trance.

– Anna. Anna, what's going on? Why are you lettin' this 'appen?

Anna smiles. A mother's smile of exaggerated sympathy. A sarcasm to increase the creeping terror. The shadow's fingers end their slow stroking and stop just below his ribcage. Carl feels a pressure, then intense pain, as the shadow hand goes in through the flesh. He feels it pass through his chest and grip his beating heart with an icy grasp. Anna shifts nervously, dribbling, rubbing herself through her skirt. Drool runs down her chin and hangs in long drips to her breasts. Her eyes are glazed. Carl feels his heart pulled down and out of him, sees it held up by the shadow. There is silence, and then, as the shadow bites into the pumping muscle, screams erupt from all around, unseen beings howl and shriek. The shadow stands and light bursts from his face and a glow shines around him like a halo, spreading out. Anna's image stutters and fades, then vanishes and the room is filled with a light too bright to look at.

Watched through the spyhole, five locks turn catches and the door swings open.

– Easy, Padre.

– What's 'appening, Blue?

Clarence locks all five latches. They sound loud in the quiet. He shows Carl through to the living room. Several men sitting around on the sofa and chairs. Smoke heavy in the air.

– Can I 'ave a word in private?

Clarence nods at the kitchen and leads Carl through, shutting the door behind him.

– Wha's goin' on, Carl? I heard you beat up a friend'a mine.

– He deserved it.

– Said you attacked 'im unexpected. Beat 'im bad.

– He give me fuckin' attitude 'ere. He was starin' at me, kissin' 'is teeth at me in the street. Fuck 'im.

– I can't do business with you, if ya goin' round fightin' my boys.

– Some'a your boys tried to rob me.

– What?

– You 'eard. I wanna hear it from your mouth, that you had nothing to do with it.

– Why ya say that? Me an' you go back long time.

– I know, Clarence, but things are gettin' messy.

– Maybe them think you deserve it?

– Maybe I do. What are you gonna do about it?

– Nothin'. I heard they got hurt pretty bad anyway.

– So, you do know about it?

– I heard about somethin'. I didn't know it was you. Them are mash up bad. In a hospital, fucked up.

– Good. They had guns. I ran 'em over.

Clarence offers Carl a go on his joint, but Carl shakes his head. Clarence takes a deep pull on it, holds it down a moment, then lets the smoke drift slowly from his mouth and nose.

– What you wan' me to do?

– You better get your boys straightened out. Everyone's on edge. It was Mick's parcels I was movin'. If I tell Mick what happened, all kinds of hell is gonna break loose. You gonna sort it, or am I tellin' Mick?

– You don't 'ave to tell no one. I'll deal with it.

– Good. Now let's see if any'a your boys is gonna gimme attitude. If one'a them looks me in the eye, I'm gonna shoot 'em in the fuckin' face.

Carl shows Clarence the gun.

– Carl, you gettin' crazy.

Carl walks back through the living room. Nobody looks at him.

CARL PULLS UP IN A PARKING SPACE AND WATCHES A GREY CLOUD cross the deep blue above. A shadow moves over the tarmac, bricks and concrete. A row of houses opposite an industrial plant. Youths on the street corner, smoking. The shadow eclipses the lads and their eyes disappear in the black shade of their hoods.

Carl gets out of the car. Five fellas staring. Carl holds eyes on one of them as he struts past, then crosses the road and walks towards the third house in. Doorbell chimes a sad sound, like the batteries are dying, and the door opens onto a dark hallway, smell of curry. Carl sits with Hamid and four others on a sofa and chairs in a room last decorated in the fifties. Hamid sits forward to face Carl.

– Yes, Uncle.

– What's happenin', Uncle?

– All good, all good.

– How's the family?

– Good, Uncle.

– Sweet.

– I'm sorry for your brother.

– Yeah, cheers.

– I heard you have stopped and now you come back.

– Yeah.

Hamid smiles. It's not a friendly smile, or a happy smile, but a smile that he thinks is expected. A mask. Carl looks at it, wondering what is behind. The others all wear blank faces without expression.

– You know anything about them killins?

– Everybody talk about killing everybody. No, no killing.

– No one knows who done 'em.

– No, nobody knows.

– Some'a your lot got done.

– Yes. I think it's them black bastards.

– Why d'ya think that?

– Don't know. They always make problems.

– Some'a theirs got done 'n all.

– Yes.

– Fuck knows.

– Fuck knows, but everyone wants to shoot each other now.

– Yeah.

– What you want, Uncle? You didn't come to ask stupid questions, no?

– Na. Sort me out. Same as always, boss.

Hamid nods at a younger fella Carl doesn't recognise and he leaves the room. Hamid sits staring at Carl with the same fake smile as before. Carl looks round the room. Everything neat and tidy. Nothing looks decrepit, but the décor and furniture are all old.

The younger man comes back into the room and puts a packet in front of Hamid. Hamid opens it and passes it to Carl.

Very good.

– No doubt, boss.

Carl closes the parcel and they count out the money. Carl looks round the room as Hamid checks it, and all four of the others are looking at the cash. He already has a device in his hand. Carl sits forward and drops it. He shifts in his seat and kicks it under the sofa.

– All good?

– Yes, Uncle.

– Right, I'll be off then.

– Goodbye.

– See you later.

The young one sees Carl out the door.

Carl walks out into the street, strange atmosphere of aggravation and malice rising off the houses and the road. The youths stare Carl down and he looks back for a few moments, then looks away. One of the boys steps forward, emboldened by Carl looking away.

– What'a you lookin' at?

– You what?

Carl stops walking.

– Who are you lookin' at?

– You fuckin' what?

Carl starts walking at the boy, mad stare of rage and violence. The boy backtracks, looking worried, wishing he hadn't started. He puts a hand in his back pocket, as though to pull a knife. Carl stops.

– Yeah, thought so. Frightened of fists. Fuckin' pussy.

Carl gets in the car, looks back at the youths, fires up the engine and pulls away.

– D'YA WANNA COME UP?

– Yeah.

– Come on then.

Anna takes Shane's hand and leads him into the building and up the stairs.

– Lift not working?

– I'm on the first floor. I hope you're not lazy.

She opens the door and pulls him in. Shuts the door and kisses him like a predator pouncing on its prey. Unzips her skirt and lets it fall to the floor. Shoves him against the wall and unbuttons his fly. She grabs hold of his cock between forefinger and thumb and leads him to the living room.

– Be rough. You can slap me and push me about a bit. Hold me by the throat.

– Whoa, steady on.

– What's the matter?

– I don't know. Slow down a bit.

– What's wrong with you? You a man or what?

– Yeah, but.

– D'you know what, forget it.

Shane stands there with his cock hanging out, wishing he hadn't said anything. Anna shoves him back and then slaps him.

– Go on. Fuck off. What are you standing there like an idiot for? Fuck off.

Shane tucks himself back in.

– Fuckin' hell, Anna. You're fucking mad.

– Get out!

– Jesus.

He leaves the door open. Anna sits down and sobs into

her hands. The sobs turn into a giggle. She wipes her tears and starts laughing. She laughs for some time.

– Fuckin' useless.

LATE-NIGHT VISIT. DANCE OF SLOW STRIPTEASE. SHE WINDS HER hips in a mesmeric sway. Eerie vision in soft haze. Ghost-girl strut, losing layers. Wrap-around skirt undone and floats off flimsy in the dim light. Sheer shirt unbuttoned in rhythm of cat-like prance and floats away to chase the skirt on a breeze and settle together in the dark corner of a bad-dream room. Carl in a trance on the sofa, watching. Predator front of unsuspecting prey. Hypnotised by a spectral dream creature, fantastic display. Ready to strike at any moment. Winding, snake-like and sprung. Pretty tits, no bra, just a tiny see-through piece of cloth, tied together at the sides. The predator holds the prey in fixed stare of fire eyes. Lit up from the inside, unearthly being. And as her halo burns, she pulls at the ribbons. The bows undo and come apart, and the shimmering gossamer floats away to join the rest of the discarded clothes. The girl glows bright, alive with lust and power. Carl licks his lips as the show goes on. Slick wraith whirl, succubus seductress. Sublime priestess of sacred blue ritual.

In a dim booth at the back of the pub, Mick and Carl watch the barmaid collect glasses.

– That's alright, ain't it?

– Yeah. Very nice.

The girl bends over and Mick raises his eyebrows, blows air through his lips like a silent whistle.

– I need you to do a bit'a work for me.

– What's up wi' your boys?

– Busy. I'll sort you out, don't worry. It's only a pickup and drop. Local.

– How much?

– A monkey.

– Alright. I'll do it.

– Good lad.

– What d'ya want me to do?

– Pick up a parcel from this address and take it to Garry.

Mick hands Carl a piece of paper with an address on it.

– Alright, Mick. Do you want me to let you know when I'm done?

– Yeah. Give me a bell.

– When d'ya want it done?

– Tomorrow. I'll bell ya when it's ready. Want another one?

– Na, I'm alright with this, mate.

Carl knocks back the rest of his pint, while Mick stares at him.

– Nothing come up on your recordings then?

– Na. There's fuckin' loads left to listen to though. Takes hours.

– Yeah.

– Any news? I ain't heard nothing for a few days.

– No, nothing.

The room gets darker. Mick, like a monster in shadow. Heavy brow and cheeks lit. Eyes black.

– Got another little job for ya, if you want it.

– What's that?

– Remember Trevor?

– Yeah.

– He's getting on me nerves.

– Oh yeah?

– Yeah. Getting a bit cocky. Needs taking down a peg or two. He wants reminding who's who.

– What d'ya want doin'?

– Graham is takin' a few parcels over his place on Friday. He's gonna 'ave cash there. I want the paper and the parcels. You take half the gear if it comes off. Come and see me tomorrow after the drop if you need a shooter.

– Got a shooter plotted up somewhere.

– Good. Don't let 'im get near ya. He ain't no mug. Make sure ya tap 'im up 'n all.

– Might need a motor.

– No probs.

– And a driver.

– Fuckinell, you want me to do it for ya?

– No. You want *me* to do it for *you*.

Mick laughs and his monstrous features expand and distort in the shade of the low light. The laugh echoes and fills Carl's mind. The face before him blurs into meaningless shapes.

EMPTY BUILDINGS OF AN OLD, DISUSED INDUSTRIAL ESTATE. CARL watching a shadow move across the face of a derelict workshop. Looks up to the white disc, eternal light ablaze in the blue. Tall windows smashed, some boarded over. Muntin squares of glass, reflecting sky interrupted by broken black holes. Somebody watching. He feels those terrible eyes bore into him. Ruined brick warehouse and factory ghosts. Sad silence of long-stopped work. Emptiness of no machines and the spaces where they once stood. Quiet road between. Carl walks along the grey loneliness of abandoned foundries, unsure why he's here. Can't remember. Desolation of derelict depots and old empty plants. Above tall buildings the clouds move fast. Malevolent atmosphere of alien forces.

Rusting metal sliding door pulled slightly ajar. Movement inside catches Carl's eye and he walks towards it. Darkness within. Mystery of an unknown world. He heaves the heavy door and it groans in its track, then stops, jammed. Enough to squeeze through. Inside, a vast space, pillars rising to high ceiling. A feeling of being watched, more intense with every step. He walks towards some office rooms at the far side. Echo of footsteps in the cold emptiness. As he reaches the smaller rooms, movement at the edge of his eye again, in the endless taper of a long corridor to his right. He looks round in time to see a woman disappear through a doorway. Stockings, heels, but that's all. Her nudity, soft against the hard, brick walls and iron rails. He follows her down the corridor. The hallway, so long it feels like it goes on forever. The door at the other end stretching into the distance. As he walks towards it, it seems further away.

A scraping sound from the big room. He looks back and the corridor, so long, the large room he came from, so far.

A figure walking in his direction behind him. A shadow man. Silhouette of spectral pursuit, he turns and walks, quick pace. He reaches the door at the end and goes through. An iron staircase rising to another level. Far up into the haze of sunlit dust. Beams of light through high windows. He hears the echo of heels on metal steps and looks up. Above him, the nude girl ascends. Stocking tops and thighs give way to flashes of in-between. She vanishes into the mist of dust. Carl looks down the corridor to see the dark figure approaching, rapid. He climbs the stairs.

Pulling himself up with the help of a metal banister, he takes three steps at a time. Some missing, or broken, but he leaps them easily enough. As he reaches the top, there is a platform, like a gangway, railings either side. The naked girl turns a corner and is gone again. Carl looks down to see the shadow climbing. He runs along the platform and turns at the end, in time to see the girl slip through another doorway ahead. He follows her into the darkness.

The darkness reaches shadow hands that hold Carl, seizing him by his arms and hair and throat. He's held still, forced to witness. A tall and destitute being with a paper bag on his head, face drawn on in felt tip, raises its hands and speaks in alien language. Unknown words, intoxicating, delirious. The air changes and Carl feels a surge of euphoria. A fever lights the atmosphere and a mesmerised crowd of vagabonds appear from the gloom, sway with ecstasy. A group in filthy rags drag a girl in a white smock to where the tall being stands. She looks frightened as they approach. The tall creature's drawn-on mask changes to a horrible grin. He touches the girl on the forehead and a circular symbol appears in red. He points to her smock and she struggles as the others forcibly remove it, pleading and crying. The fight goes out of her as the clothing is lost. The naked girl is held prone. The tall one removes the paper bag from his head to reveal a round, flat, spiral face, like a lollipop. He positions himself behind the girl and holds her by the hips. She pushes back against his thrusts and her eyes light up like fire. She has a halo and the light from her eyes glows on the idiot faces of the vagrant crowd.

When they are finished, the girl gives a signal and the tall man is seized. He struggles and fights as he is stripped of his clothes. They hold him before her stretched out and the girl, directing it all, has a sharp stone raised like a trophy. Its shiny black surface catches the light in her eyes. She lowers it and draws it across his torso, just below the ribs. He opens to her hand and she reaches inside. His heart is removed, and she brings it to her lips. She kisses the beating core and the man fades to nothing. The girl holds the still-pumping muscle up and a peculiar light glows inside it. The light grows brighter and becomes intense and the others fall to their knees in awe.

LYING STILL, CARL ON A SOFA, STARING INTO NOWHERE. TWO AND A half hours in a black hole. Dark vortex of paralysis. The black nothing enveloping him in the void. Fall into abyss. Can't move, can't think. Lost. Non-day. Missing. The whole afternoon, gone.

The day had started out alright. A few missions. A pick-up, a drop. Couple of phone calls. Carl stopped at the supermarket to grab a few bits. It was in there things started to deteriorate. Android spies. Weird light. Endless boxes and tins and cartons. Looks of judgement. Disapproval. He had to escape. Abandoned the trolley and left with nothing. Had to get home. He couldn't look anyone in the eye.

Then the signal started. Invisible, alien beam projected into his mind. Disrupted thoughts. Glitched visions. Stolen, replaced. He wished Anna was there.

Trying to watch a documentary about military invasion to distract. But the beam is transmitted on the back of the TV signal. Psychic attack. Winged creatures, diving. Torment.

A rectangle appears in the air. Between the sofa and the television. Translucent. Hanging there, floating. About a metre or so wide and a bit less tall. Another screen. Frenetic fuzz of interference. Then it changes. Shimmers with light. Like the reflections of a swimming pool on a ceiling. It looks as though it's made of nothing but moving light. Small luminous waves and ripples. Carl stares at it in wonder. It might be a doorway. A way out. To escape the suffocation of everyday existence. It's this or the noose. A portal into another world. If he climbs into it, will he be free? What's on the other side? He hesitates, watching it glimmer in the room. The rectangle is gone. Too late. He missed it. He missed his chance.

Or did he?

Drift delirious, detached desolation. Swallows pills to murder the harpies.

Sirens get louder then fade away. A flock of birds fly from a roof. The sun sits low behind a streaked cloud, like a scar across the eye. Carl, sitting on a low wall, watches a shadow cross the street towards him. A car pulls up. Window down. Darren grinning wide under mirror shades. Carl looks in, sees himself twice in the sunglasses.

– Alright, mate.

– Easy.

– You need a ride.

– Yeah.

– Jump in.

•

Parked up in a dull street. Radio low. Irritation of bad songs and mindless talk. Darren adding to the dreary din with inane chat of meaningless trivial rubbish, invading Carl's consciousness like a psychic attack. The sound of the radio mixing with Darren's words drilling deeper into Carl's brain. Wriggling in his mind like an unscratchable itch. Anxiety rising. Quiet street of still calm outside the car. Pressure building. Carl leans forward and pulls the pistol from a bag in the footwell.

– …and she says to Bob…

– Shut the fuck up, you're drivin' me round the fuckin' bend.

– Alright, mate, take it easy. I'm just tryin' ta pass the time.

Carl stares at Darren, pressed against the door, fear in his eyes. He lowers the gun back to his lap, pointing it at the glovebox.

– And turn that fuckin' shit off.

Darren switches off the radio and they both sit looking out the windscreen at the grey street in silence. Slow, soundless minutes.

– Are you alright? D'you want me ta come in wiv ya?

– Na. I told ya. When the other fella turns up, I'm gonna steam in behind 'im. I gotta time it just right. You sit tight. Keep the engine runnin'. When I come out, throw it in gear with the clutch down. Don't fuckin' stall it. I want you ready to pull away before I get the door shut.

– Alright, mate. I done this before.

A cat crosses the road. Stops halfway, looking around, then runs under a parked car. An old lady walks round the corner and disappears down an alley between houses. A car passes slow. The driver stares at Darren as he goes by. Then silence again. A long quiet. Distant sound of traffic. Clouds move across the sky. Carl sees a shadow fall across the house he's going to. A car pulls up. A man gets out carrying a sports bag.

– That's him.

Carl pulls the peak low, scarf up over nose, gets out and slow walks up a drive two doors up, looking the other way. He pretends to knock and waits with his back to the man, as he knocks at the target's door. He turns to face forward, watching out the corner of his eye. Trevor answers, lets Graham in. As he puts a foot across the threshold, Carl bolts across the drive, low wall, front garden, without slowing slams into the back of Graham, sending him falling onto Trevor, and they both stumble, Trever falling back and Graham tripping over him. They look up to see a man pointing a pistol at them. Baseball cap down, scarf up. Mad eyes between.

– Stay on the fuckin' floor.

– Whatever you think you're doin', you better think twice, boy. You're a fuckin' dead man.

– Shut ya fuckin' mouth. You. Kick the bag over 'ere.

Graham pushes it towards Carl with his foot.

– You. Where's the fuckin' money?

– Fuck off.

– I ain't fuckin' about. Where's the money?

– In there. Sideboard. Top drawer.

– Get up. Walk in slow.

Trevor and Graham get up and walk to the front room. Trevor goes for his pocket and Carl pulls the trigger. A loud bang in the small hall, ears ringing. Trevor falls to his knees and keels over, clutching at his thigh, above the knee. Graham holding his hands to his ears, flinching, grimace of fear.

– Get the fuckin' dough, or I'll put one in you 'n all.

Carl can hear his own voice from a long way off, through the shrill tone in his ears. He follows Graham. Standing in the doorway, one eye on Trevor in the hall, one eye on Graham in the front room. He drops a bug and kicks it under the sofa. Everything slow motion. Graham pulling a big envelope from a drawer.

– Chuck it 'ere and get on the floor.

Graham does as he's told. Carl steps back out into the hall, puts the envelope in the bag with the gear. He walks out and slams the door. Neighbours in the street, wondering where the gunshot came from. Looking at him as he gets in the car.

– Drive.

Carl watching the street. Nothing happens. He realises the engine isn't running. Angry, he turns in his seat to see a terrified woman pressed up against the door. He looks down at the gun in his hand and the open bag, money and drugs.

– Sorry. Wrong motor.

He jumps back out as Trevor's door opens and sees Darren looking confused three cars down. Same car, same colour. He runs over and gets in, Darren taking off as he sits. He shuts the door as they speed away.

– What happened?

– I shot 'im.

– I guessed that. I meant gettin' in that other car.

Carl starts to laugh. He laughs for a long time.

Spectral spectator. Not present. Watching, like a film. The world around him, a dull sound from a long way off. Muted, muffled. Vision distorted. Faces shifting form. Changing. Fading out to revolting masks. Becoming part of the background. Blurring to nothing but dark and light. Disappearing completely. Speed-dial dreaming. Third-eye navigation of the unsolid sights, floating through the moon's watch of the no-time, in a nowhere night.

– WHAT D'YA MEAN IT WAS YOU SHOT 'IM?

– It was me. He went for 'is pocket.

– You robbed my gear?

– You told me to.

– No I fuckin' didn't. I told you to do a couple of pickups and drops for me, nothin' else.

– What? You told me to rob Graham and Trevor 'n all. You told me Trev was getting too big for 'is boots. Said I could keep half the gear. You sorted me a driver for it.

– What'a you fuckin' talkin' about? The driver was for running about. You were meant to get a bit of gear off Trevor and lay a bug there.

– Why'a you lyin'?

– You what? Where are ya? You're fuckin' dead, boy.

Carl ends the call. It doesn't make sense. He looks at the window. The curtains are closed. A glow of dim light around them and through the narrow gap between. All the light in the room is sucked out through the curtains. He sits in a shadow haze.

He goes through the remembered conversation in his head. Dark booth at the back of the pub. Mick's big, square face. Huge hands on the table. Monster in the dull light. He knows he heard those words. Why was Mick doing this? Now what?

Carl looks in the bag. A lot of money with the gear. The dough must be fifty grand on its own. He thinks about the attempt on him the other day. The lads who tried to take him in the car park. Was that a set-up from Mick too? Who knows what? Did Graham and Trevor know he was coming?

The phone rings again. It's Anna. Carl doesn't know if he can trust her. He throws the phone across the room.

A reflex response. It's still ringing. He crosses the room and picks it up.

– Anna?

– Carl? Are you alright?

– Na.

– What's wrong?

– Everything's gone tits up.

– I heard you were having a bit of trouble.

– Just a bit.

– D'you want me to come round?

– No. No I don't want you here. I've gotta go.

– Why? Where are you goin'?

– I'm gonna disappear.

– Carl, don't do that.

– Why?

– I can't help you if you vanish.

– What are you gonna do?

– I can sort things out. With Mick. Smooth it over.

– I don't want nothing to do with that cunt. Why are you close to 'im? You tell me not to get involved. I've had enough.

– Carl... wait...

– I don't want nothing to do with you either.

– Carl—

Carl ends the call. It rings again, but he dumps it. He stares at the phone for some time. Like he might see the answer in it. Nothing. Only lights in a screen. He realises they're all in it together. Mick, Anna, all of them. Trying to confuse him. He looks back in the bag. He hasn't got long. He goes to the bedroom and throws a pile of clothes on the bed. Couple of pairs of jeans, couple of shirts, a few T-shirts, a hoodie and all the pants and socks in his drawer. He grabs a big sports bag, scoops up all the clothes and shoves them in it. Goes back to the living room and grabs the bag with the bricks and the money. He finds his own money he'd stashed up too. Puts on a coat in the hall. Out on the landing, down the stairs. He hesitates to look round the car park before he steps out.

Carl lobs the bags in the back of the motor and jumps in. He turns the engine over and pulls away. He has to get away from here. To disappear. He looks at the block of flats getting smaller in the rear-view. Feels nothing. Never has the attachment other people seem to develop to places they live in. One place is as good as the next. As long as he has somewhere to put his head down, everything's alright. He smiles to himself.

He turns onto the main road. The flats are behind a row of houses. They dissolve in the grey sky. Black cloud moves across the thick atmosphere. A shadow follows him along the road and falls across the houses he is passing. Carl looks across the rec. The girl is there, but without her son. He pulls up in a space at the kerb and gets out of the car. He watches her from a distance. Short skirt, low-cut top. Ankle boots with a heel. He takes it all in. She turns her head towards him, and they look at each other for a long time. Carl walks through the gate and makes his way over to the bench.

– Where's the boy?

– I'm not allowed to see him.

– Why?

– Not fit to be a mother, apparently. I lost access.

– What's your name?

– Jane.

– Jane. You wanna go for a little adventure?

– Where?

– Dunno yet. Just get in a car and drive. Don't know when I'm coming back.

– Yeah. Why not.

– Come on then. Let's go.

– Can we drop by mine to pick up a few bits and bobs?

Carl turns and walks back to the car. Jane follows.

– We gotta be quick at yours. I need to get out of 'ere, fast.

They drive round the corner to her place and Carl waits in the car. Looking out at the street, he wishes he'd gone inside with her. Someone could see him here. Jane comes out with a small case and Carl throws it in the boot. Back out on the main road, he feels the weightless sense of freedom and adventure flow through his veins. They both sit there smiling at the streets they leave behind.

Carl turns onto the dual carriageway and slides in between two cars, smooth and fluid motion. He guns it up to fifty, takes a deep breath and sighs heavily. He feels free. A chuckle escapes his lips. He knows other people are never this free. So attached to things and jobs and other people in a way he couldn't be even if he wanted to. He starts to laugh. It goes on some and he can't remember why he is laughing. Jane looks at him, unsure of what's funny. But she joins in and they both laugh together as the car sings along.

Street lights and signs fly past and the road disappears beneath them. Buildings drift by. Housing estates, high-rises, industrial estates. Every one containing a different reality. Different rules of life. Different lies. Then fields. The fields seem to float away, giving Carl a feeling of flight.

THROUGH BROKEN TOWN, OLD BUILDINGS. DECAY, DERELICTION. Abandoned houses. Run-down shops and nothing decorated or maintained for a long time. Jane and Carl are silent. A gap between buildings shows the sea and Carl feels a sense of arrival. He never lived by the sea, but whenever he sees it, he feels at home. Like he had been close to the shore-lapping waves in another life.

Carl pulls up outside a scruffy bed and breakfast. A rooming house. Cheap place to put his head down, 'til something else works out. He gets out of the car and leans in through the open window.

– Wait here while I check it out.

The door has a big, old-style knocker that looks like it'll come off if it's banged too hard. Up close, the front of the place is dilapidated. A poor state of disrepair. An old lady opens the door. Inside, smell of damp wood, old fifties décor. Nothing touched for years. They agree a price for the room and she fusses over him like an old aunt.

Carl pins her up against the wall, kissing her wrinkled skin and round the mouth, licking off the dry spittle in the corner of her lips. A hand pulling up her skirt to get at her dry old quim behind those big, greying pants with yellow stains. He sees her blinking at him, waiting for an answer to whatever she'd just asked him.

– Sorry. I drifted off then. Long drive. What did you say?

– Don't worry, dear. You sit down. I'll make you a cuppa. I only asked if you want to see the room, before you decide.

– Oh. Yeah, thanks.

She shows him to a room adjoining the kitchen. The kitchen is all vintage. Nothing modern. He sits at a table and watches her make tea. Her humming an ancient tune. Steam from an ancient kettle. It whistles and the shrill sound shatters the quiet of the still afternoon. The sound of pouring water. Tinkling of a teaspoon in the mug as she hums. He drinks his tea while she chatters on about the weather and other mundane things he can't be bothered to listen to. He looks at her face and it grows, elongated and severe. The distortion turning her into an old witch, a demonic being. Carl looks at his tea, wonders if it's poisoned, has a sip and when he looks back at her, she's a friendly little old lady again.

In the bedroom, she shows him an old double bed, a small desk with a chair and, between several rows of houses, a sea view. A narrow view, but he feels comforted by the sight of it. Like knowing it's there offers him some sort of protection against the forces that try to crush him. He stares at it between buildings. The old woman is talking. He has no idea what she's been saying. He looks round the shabby room and back at the thin strip of sea.

– I'll take it. Me girlfriend'll be staying for a bit.

– Oh, good boy. That's alright. I mind me own business, see, so don't mind me. You come and go as you please. You'll hardly see me.

– Thank you.

She gives him a set of keys and leaves him in the room. He realises he can't remember what she said her name was. It doesn't matter. He goes out to get Jane and the bags. Back in the room, he puts the bag with the money on top of the wardrobe. Carl looks out the window, then sits on the bed. He lies back with his hands behind his head and watches the sky. A dark cloud slides through the blue and throws the room into shadow. Jane stands at the end of the bed, looking at him.

ANNA IS LOOKING OUT HER WINDOW. SHE IS NAKED. THE WINDOW IS open and the curtains blow and flap around her face. She sees Carl below, walking towards the block of flats. He presses the door entry button. A loud buzzing noise fills her ears. She goes to answer the entry handset and the abrasive noise continues until she lifts the receiver.

– Hello, Carl.

– Hello, Anna.

– Do you want to see me?

– Yes.

She presses a button. Carl at the main door fades to nothing. Reappears on the landing, at the top of the stairs. She sees him approach through the spyhole. He knocks at the door and the knocking is loud. It echoes through the building. The spyhole becomes an eye, looking at him. The door opens. He walks into the living room and Anna glides in. Her bare skin glows with pulsing light from within and her halo is bright. She passes Carl a dark, viscous drink. He sips at it and the taste is harsh, like strong medicine mixed with alcohol. He holds it to the light, then knocks back some more. Grimaces as he swallows it down. A light fires up in Anna's eyes and she smiles. Her smile is frightening. Carl's eyes turn black. He looks at her nudity. His eyes travel down, over her breasts, and settle at her sex. It seems to throb with a great energy and he stares, mesmerised. She whispers his name and his eyes move back to her smile.

– Drink.

The liquid voice is in his mind. Anna speaks without moving her lips. He drinks the rest and hands her back the empty glass. The air swirls around him in slow eddies and currents. He sees it move. The atmosphere changes colour.

Carl kisses Anna on the lips. He then walks round her and stops behind. Parting the hair on the back of her head, he finds another face. The face identical to the face on the front of Anna's head. He kisses that too.

She turns and glides out of the room. She is slightly transparent now and he sees the wall through her. She stops in the doorway and turns her head. Two eyes aflame and a third in her forehead, looking straight through him. She disappears and reappears in one-second intervals, fading each time, until nothing is there.

Carl looks at an old sideboard. On it are strange little apothecary bottles with coloured liquids and powders, a dagger, a half-burnt photograph of a man with the eyes scratched out and a saucer containing a small pile of ashes. A drawer opens and Carl looks inside. Sealer bags with cuttings of hair and fingernails, some wax figurines. Each one has a photograph stuck on the face. He sees Mick's face on one of the dolls. There are several others with faces he recognises as victims of the murders. There is a hole in each of their chests, where the heart would be. Carl sees another at the back of the drawer. It's face down and its hands are tied behind its back. He goes to lift the poppet out and look at it. See its face. But he stops. Hand hovering over it. He leaves it there, face down.

DEAN TIES OFF A ROPE ON A RAFTER ABOVE THE LOFT HATCH. HE puts the noose over his head, around his neck. A tear rolls down his cheek. There's nothing left for him here. He sees the setting sun in the bedroom window, through an open door. The red disc looks back. All-seeing eye. It shimmers in the haze of city pollution. Its rays fill the room with a golden light that promises magic. Dean kicks the stool away. He jerks and struggles. Then falls limp. Swaying gently.

Carl watches. Unable to stop it. He shouts at Dean, but the scream is silent. Dean doesn't respond. There's nothing he can do. Carl watches again, from the beginning of the scene. He shouts at Dean to stop, but no sound comes out. Dean setting up the rope. He can't see or hear Carl. He puts the noose over his head and takes a last look at the sun. Carl crying. Helplessly watching his brother's end. Over and over on a loop.

STANDING AT THE EDGE, LOOKING OUT, CARL SEES THE ABYSS. THE place where the water meets heaven is obscured in blurred mist. The sky dissolves into the sea. No horizon. Unreachable threshold. Mystic greys, blues, greens. Impossible colour. The way it shimmers and glistens and sparkles where the sun catches the surface whenever it comes out from behind the clouds. Endless black, when the light is dull. So much of it. All that water across the globe. So deep. The tide coming in and going out with the pull of the moon.

Carl feels the great power of the sea. The incredible destruction and creation of its force. Where natural and supernatural are the same thing. The word *awesome* is overused to the point of no effect, but the sea is truly awe-inspiring. He feels his insignificance. Knowing he is tiny in this world and nothing amongst the stars.

Carl sees himself, tossed on the crests, smashed against rocks. Drowning. The waves lap at the shore. They burst on the water withdrawing and crawl up the wet sand to almost touch his toes. Sometimes coming further to soak his feet. A few yards out, the sea is chaotic. He thinks about wading in. To walk out until he is consumed by the waves. Pulled down into the cold, black depths.

Jane is standing nearby, watching a gull hover. The bird swoops and dives. She looks along the desolate beach. Deserted sand. Lonely promenade. Insistent call of hungry gulls. Looking for their moment.

– Can we go back?

– Yeah. Come on, let's go.

She takes his hand and they walk back across the beach. Carl stops and looks back at the sad sun, burning a halo on low clouds above the dim horizon. Jane waits, looking at him watching the sky and the sea. He turns and they stroll back to the guest house.

Inside the gloom of the room, Carl stands at the mirror, staring at his reflection. Jane sitting on the bed, watching.

– What are you doing?

– Have you ever looked into your own self, 'til everything else disappears, leaving your eyes floating in nothing?

– No.

– You should.

– Why?

– To enter the mysteries. The abyss.

– None of this seems real.

– What?

– Us, being here. It's strange.

– It ain't real, is it?

– Feels like a dream.

– Yeah. And yet, at the same time, everything else has vanished. Like when I stare into my own eyes.

Carl is lost in his reflection. Jane drifts into her own thoughts.

– You never asked me why I can't see my child.

– I did. You said you lost access.

– But, I mean, you never asked why I lost access.

– I don't care. You can tell me if you want. I won't judge.

– I don't want to. It just seems strange you didn't ask.

– People want to know everyone's business. Nosey fuckers. You are what you are.

– Yeah.

– You ain't no good?

– So they say.

– That's good enough.

– Is that a compliment?

– If ya like.

Carl lies on the bed next to Jane. He leans his head on her lap.

– I'm going nowhere. You wanna come?

– Yeah. Why not?

– That's nice enough for me.

Sitting on the bed, Jane stroking Carl's hair. She smiles.

– Would you like me to tell you a story?

– Yeah.

– Alright. A wolf walks alone through the trees. He is hunting. Sunbeams reach the forest floor through the branches and leaves here and there. A girl is picking wild flowers for her grandmother. The wolf watches her from behind an old oak. Below her red cloak, her long legs are slender and coltish. The wolf licks his lips. He dreams of licking her all over.

– I like it.

– Good. The girl walks into the woods and the cool air of the shade feels good on her bare legs. The wolf steps out from his hiding place. Where are you going, girl? I'm going to visit my grandmother. What lovely flowers. Are they for her? Yes. You are a sweet girl. Do you have far to go? She lives in a house at the back of the woods. Good day to you, girl. I'll see you around. Good day, Mr Wolf.

– Nice.

– Yeah. I'm good at stories.

– So it seems.

– The wolf walks back off along the path, into the trees. He'd seen an old house at the back of the woods before. That must be it. He runs unseen through forest, dodging trees and thickets until he reaches the old house. He knocks at the door. An old lady answers and the wolf takes her down. The wolf kills her quick and has his fill. He puts on her clothes and waits for the girl.

– I like it.

– Stop interrupting.

– Sorry.

– Soon there comes a knock at the door. Come in, sweet girl. Hello Grandmother. Good day, my sweet child. My, what a big tongue you have. All the better to lick you with. My, what big hands you have. All the better to feel you with. The wolf lifts his dress. My, what a big cock you have. All the better to fuck you with. The wolf springs forward and catches the girl. He pushes her over the bed and sweeps aside her red cloak. He yanks up her skirt and whisks her knickers down. The girl, prone, waits, eager for whatever will come next. The wolf looks at her beautiful skin. So soft. He licks up the crease and runs his long tongue all over her cheeks and between her legs. She squirms and giggles as the wolf holds her hips and pushes himself in.

– You got my blood goin', I'm hard.

– I haven't finished. When they are done, the wolf turns to leave, but the girl pulls a big stone from the pocket of her cloak and cracks it into the side of his skull. He falls to the floor and lies there moaning. The girl takes a knife and cuts him below the ribs. She reaches inside and finds his beating heart. Pulls it free and takes a bite. Blood pools around the wolf as she gobbles it down. She smiles to herself. Everything turned out just as she'd hoped.

Carl sits up and stares at Jane. He frowns. She looks back and smiles. There's a long silence.

– You ruined it.

He gets up and walks round the small room. She watches him pace, amused at his confusion. He's irritated. Something feels wrong. Why did she spoil the ending? He looks back at the bed and Anna is sitting there, grinning. She opens her mouth and inside is a chaos. Destruction. Anna becomes Jane again. A shadow spreads out from the corner of the skirting, up across the wall, and swallows the room.

Jane gets up off the bed and grabs Carl by his collar and kisses him with a forceful passion. Groping through his trousers, as he stands there, accepting it. She pulls away and slaps his face.

– You dirty bastard.

He grins. She throws herself, face down, bent over on the bed, feet on the floor, and pulls up her skirt. No knickers. She shuffles her legs apart and sticks her arse out, pushing it up in the air and wriggling it, as though rubbing it on something invisible. Humping the air.

Carl stands to one side, a hand on the back of her neck, and brings his other hand down hard on the bare cheeks. Over and over. Pink and sore, Jane moans softly and pushes back at the sting. He opens his fly and gets behind her. Wet. Slides in. Transfers the spectre. Puts the monsters in her. The darkness. Poisons her. She bucks and sways. He pants and jags. She is Anna again. Undulating rhythm. Winding hips. Slow grind. Eyes alight. Frenzied fuck to the finish.

They lie there, gasping for air. Soft explosion in the bone box. Fire flow through the blood. The ceiling breathes and shudders. The walls are alive. Colours are brighter. Nothing is said. No need for words. Nothing matters.

GRAHAM UNLOCKS THE DOOR AND WALKS IN. DARK HALL. QUIET. Distant sound of outdoors. He looks through the kitchen and the back door is open. Gut drops through a trapdoor. Hears a sound behind him, movement at the edge of his eye. Too late. A heavy blow to the side of his head. Silent, he falls down in the darkness. Down and down into nowhere. The black nothing envelops him. He can't move. His clothes come away, releasing him. Floating. The beat of his heart, echoing in the dull thud of a deep ache in the skull. Nausea. A sharp cut below his ribs. Blurred vision of a creature reaching into him and pulling out his core. A pulsing light. Then darkness again.

– So you don't know where he is?

– No.

– No idea?

– Not a Danny.

Mick grabs Anna's face, squeezing her cheeks, and shoves her against the wall.

– If I find out you're lying t'me.

Anna looks at him with detached, blank eyes. Her apathy unnerves him. He lets go of her face. Anna wipes the smell of his hand off her mouth.

– I ain't fuckin' about, Anna. You'n 'im were close. He trusts you.

– I know. I'm sorry. I can't help you.

– I want you to 'elp me. I want 'im back.

– Did you tell him to rob Trevor?

– Why d'ya say that?

– No reason.

– 'Ave you spoke to 'im?

– No. Just seems weird that he'd do it off his own back. It's not his thing, is it?

– Na. But he did it. He's unpredictable.

– I'll call him. I'll try an' find him.

– Good girl.

Anna gives Mick the doe-eyed look.

– I don't want him to die, Mick.

– He won't.

– Or get hurt too bad.

– He'll get 'urt.

– But not too bad?

– I see what I can do for ya.

– And Trevor?

– Trevor'll do as he's told.
– Thank you, Mick.

CARL KNOWS WHAT HE'S LOOKING AT SHOULD LOOK LIKE A WARDROBE. He can see the wardrobe is now a gate. The swirl of darkness moves and creaks. Gateway to chaos. Faces break out from the mass of fluid shapes. Screaming faces holler from the depths of abyss. The panic of souls consumed. Lost in the violence of unfiltered thought. Carl sits at the end of the bed, rubbing his face like he's trying to wipe the flesh off his skull. Jane asleep. Peaceful face. Carl, manic. Thoughts, a thousand miles an hour. He can't stop them. The speed increases. Beamed in from an alien entity.

He looks at Jane. So peaceful. So pretty. He wants to hurt her. To twist her head off. No, no, don't think like that. Beat her to death. The drama. The frenzy. The magic of it. The blood. The power of consuming the soul as the life is taken. No. He doesn't want to kill her. It's not her fault. There's no reason for that. He can control himself. His mind is his own. Carl is in control. Commanding his environment. The whole thing. He is making it all happen. Like the master. A puppeteer. The God.

But he's not.

Another entity is pulling the strings. Another being is directing the show.

– Kill her.

– No. Fuck off.

He sees himself running away. A giant, black head is chasing him. Mouth opening and closing. Biting at the cold black night. Chomping the air, inches from his heels. The thing grows bigger. If it catches him, he will be consumed. Obliterated. Carl knows something terrible will happen beyond his control. He turns on the beast and raises his hands. He concentrates with all his power. The monster disintegrates as it reaches him. Carl absorbs its power. He is invincible.

CARL DIALS A NUMBER AND LISTENS TO THE RINGING. IT GOES ON. As he goes to cut it off, the call is answered.

– 'Ello?

– Easy, mate. It's Carl.

– Hello Carl. How you doin'? Been a while.

– Yeah, I'm alright. You?

– Yeah, not bad. What's 'appenin'?

– I'm in your neck of the woods.

– Are ya? What brings you 'ere?

– Just 'ad to get away, ya know. Stress 'n all that.

– Yeah, I know. That's why I came out here. Bit of chill time. Escape the madness.

– Listen. Do me a favour.

– What's that?

– Don't tell no one I'm 'ere, will ya?

– No, no mate. You know me. I know that one. Secret squirrel. No worries.

– 'Ere, do you remember that fella you was saying moves a bit of this and that? The one who lives round 'ere.

– Yeah. Jack.

– Yeah, that's 'im. I got a few bits going cheap, he might be interested in.

– Oh yeah.

– Yeah. Room for you to put a bit on and still be a good little squeeze for 'im.

– Alright. I'll sort it out.

– You about later? I'll show you the bits and we'll work out a price.

– Yeah, let's do it.

– Cool. Nice one, Sean.

– No worries. Catch ya soon.

The line goes dead. Carl tries to feel pleased with himself, but there's nothing there. He looks at the room around him. The quiet sounds strange. It all seems so far away. Not just Anna, or Mick, or the trouble behind him, but the room he is in. The deal he's setting up. Even himself. The body he is in belongs to someone else. He is just an observer. Like he broke in to watch through another being's eyes. Carl doesn't exist.

•

Dean grinning. Solid image. Then fading. Solid again. Flashing. Solid. Carl knows he can make him come back. If he just concentrates hard enough. He takes a deep breath. Light flares up in the palms of his hands. Eyes alight. Fire rushing up. The room shudders and sways. Everything looks like the shimmering distortion above flames. Dean grinning. The face becomes severe. Angular. Demonic. A bird. Dean. A car. Dean. The rush explodes in his mind. A thousand voices. Screaming. Then silence. He falls forward, onto his hands and knees. Carl looks up to see the space before him, empty. A vacuum. No Dean. It didn't work. This time.

CARL LOOKS AT JANE ON THE BED WITH HER HEAD IN HER HANDS. They are a few feet apart, with an unimaginable distance between them. Removed from the room to their own infinite remoteness. Isolated. Lonely. He wonders who she is. The girl in the park. Why is she here with him? It doesn't matter. He don't know who *he* is. The room grows smaller around them, and at the same time, Jane moves further away. He sees her as though he's looking down a long tunnel with her at the other end. And then, in an instant, she is very close. Too close. He feels discomfort at her proximity and has the overwhelming need to escape the room. She looks so sad.

– You alright?

– Just missing the boy.

– Yeah.

– I shouldn't have come away. They're gonna think I don't care.

– You gotta do what you gotta do.

– I don't wanna go back.

– Yeah, I know.

– What would you do?

The room is closing in. Carl feels the air tighten around him. Jane looks strange. Her face is changing. Monstrous features. He remembers the unappealing end to her Big Bad Wolf story. Her eyes are getting bigger. Turning red, then black. The eyeballs burst and fall back into the hollow sockets. Each into an endless hole. A bottomless drop into the abyss. Through the empty sockets, he sees a small boy trying to outrun his own shadow. The dark figure on the floor bears down on him and he screams.

– I ain't gonna tell you what to do.

– What are *you* gonna do?

– I'm just gonna float about a bit.

– What does that even mean?

– Nothing. It means nothing.

Jane looks like a little girl lost. A tear runs down her cheek.

– I'm gonna go for a walk. Get a few beers, or a bottle of whisky or something.

Jane looks down and doesn't reply. She puts her head back in her hands.

– See ya in a bit.

Carl stands there a moment on the threshold, looking at Jane. He remembers her as Anna. For a moment she was Anna. Maybe she is.

– Hit her. She is bad.

No no no no.

He backs out of the room and shuts the door.

•

Along the seafront, crowded street scene. Sound of many voices mixed with cries of greedy gulls. Excited shouting, people walking towards Carl in great numbers. He struggles against the flow. Pushchairs and children. Faces appearing from the crowds, galvanised in twisted expressions. Families sat about, eating ice cream or chips. Gulls hovering, watching for an opportunity of theft. Screeching calls. Screams. A girl on a bench weeping.

In the off-licence, Carl buys a bottle of whisky. Back out on the busy road, dodging men and women, with children, bombarded by loud voices. Psychic attack. All the people become one mass, conspiring to confuse, harass, assault. They are controlled by an alien force. The mob as a single entity, directed to disturb, disrupt, dismay. A dishevelled woman in a shelter, holding a can of super-strength lager, shouting at a drunken, destitute man.

– I'll tell Jake what you said. He'll fuckin' do ya. He'll fuckin' cut ya.

– Fuck off, you old cunt. You're fuckin' mental.

Carl sees a lone figure standing still against the moving crowds of people going this way and that. It's Mick, staring at him. A solid rock in the waves. Grey cloud floats across the blue above the swirling sea. The sun is obscured and shade slides over the promenade and beach below, making Mick a shadow man.

Carl turns off the main road, up a side street. He looks back but can't see the shadow man among the throng. He crosses the road and walks into another little side street, checking over his shoulder. There's a small coffee shop along the way and Carl goes in to see if anyone is following. To catch them out. He orders a coffee and sits down, facing the window. Three spoons of sugar, slow stir. The sound of the spoon on the cup echoing in a moment of peace.

Drinking his coffee, Carl listens to the conversations around him. Whispering about him. He turns on the whisperer, an old man, who abruptly stops and stares back, indignant at the intrusion. Carl looks back to the front of the shop and watches the window. Everything is splintering, dividing. Closing in. He is the jumbled fragments of a person. Trying to remember yesterday. There are gaps. He finishes his drink and, satisfied he wasn't followed, pays and leaves.

As he turns onto another road, Carl checks over his shoulder. He's being watched. He passes a narrow street on his left and, for a moment, sees the shadow figure of Mick at the other end. Quickening his pace, he does a left, then a right, as he sees a man following him behind. He comes out on the road of the guest house he's staying at. Looking back, no one is tailing him.

Jane is not in the room. Carl shuts the door and locks it. He looks out the window. No one about. Jane has left. He knows it. He looks in the cupboard. Her clothes are gone. He drags the bag down from on top of the wardrobe. The money's still there. Carl opens the whisky and drinks from the bottle.

– Hello.

– Carl. It's Kate. Are you alright?

– Alright, sis. Yeah, I'm good.

– What happened? Where are you?

– Something went wrong. I 'ad to get a move on. I shifted out. Disappeared for a bit. I can't tell you where I am. It's better no one knows.

– Dad's worried about you.

– Serves him right.

– Carl, you can't say that. He's been through enough.

– Yeah. Well, tell 'im I'm alright then. How are you?

– Okay. Just concerned about you. You aren't well, Carl.

– I'm alright.

– Anna called. She's upset you've gone too.

– Listen, sis, I've gotta go.

– Wait, Carl. I need to sort this out.

– See ya soon.

– Carl…

•

Sitting on the bed in the small room, Carl tries to remember the day. He wonders how Anna tracked him down. Takes a long swig of whisky and passes her the bottle. She has a few gulps and passes it back.

– How have you been keeping?

– Alright. How did you find me?

– We spoke on the phone. Don't you remember?

Carl has a vague memory of the call.

– You told me where you were.

– Did I?

Carl can't take his eyes off those legs. The way they disappear up her skirt. He licks his lips and tries to focus on Anna's face.

– Yeah. Said you were hanging out with some bird from the park, I think is what you called her.

– Oh, yeah.

– Where is she?

– She's gone now.

– Well, lucky for her. I'd have slapped her up if she was here.

– You ain't got no hold on me.

– Really? Is that what you think. You don't know what's what, do you?

– Eh?

– I said, I'd still have hit her anyway.

– Oh, right.

– So, what are you gonna do?

– Dunno.

His eyes are pulled back to those smooth legs, like a magnet, leading to the bliss up her skirt.

– You should give Mick his bits back.

– Fuck him.

– Yeah, but it's for your sake.

– I don't care any more.

– You will when you're tied up and one of his goons has a pair of pliers round your balls.

Carl shifts in his seat, uncomfortable with the idea.

– Why are you so involved with Mick?

– You know I keep an eye on the clubs and bars.

– Why did you want me to stay out of it then?

– You shouldn't have got involved.

– I didn't get a say in it.

– I know. It wasn't supposed to be this way.

– What's that supposed to mean?

Anna is looking out the window. The room is in shade and her face is lit by the light coming in. She is an angel.

– I want you to come back, Carl.

– Why?

– I need you.

– You don't need anyone.

– Well then, I want you.

Anna moves, turning slightly towards him, leaving a gap between her thighs. A gateway.

– What about Mick?

– I'll sort it out with Mick. Give him the gear. You won't get hurt. I promise.

– I sold it.

– You got the money?

– Yeah.

– Good. I can work with that. You might have to take a beating.

– I'll think about it.

– I'm going back tomorrow.

– Where are you stoppin'?

– I was hoping you would have me.

Carl grins, as Anna parts her legs and gives him a better view.

SURROUNDED BY HIGH WHITE WALLS IN A WINDING CORRIDOR AMONG a queue of people. Blank faces. Everyone is wearing a simple white smock. Carl wonders where he is. There is a whirring sound. The queue moves forward. Where is it going? The corridor bends and the line of people disappears out of sight. Rising anxiety. This strange building, with its clean lines, white walls, floor and ceiling has a sinister purpose. He can sense its malice. The queue shuffles forward again. Nobody seems as concerned as he is. They are all mindless. No thought, no feeling. Like cattle for the slaughter. Carl realises that's what this is. An extermination facility. As he rounds a bend, huge glass panels come into view. Like giant aquariums. Built-in fish tanks. Large objects move a slow dance in the liquid. Despair hits him in the gut as he realises they are naked dead bodies floating, drifting past, behind the big windows. Everyone moves forward several steps. They don't notice the floating bodies.

●

Carl wakes. Anna is gone. Does she really exist? He can only believe in her when she is in front of him, solid. Sitting up in bed, he eyes the wardrobe, ominous presence. Thinks there might be somebody in it, or perhaps the cupboard itself is possessed by an evil presence. He gets out of bed and yanks the cupboard door open. Nothing.

Maybe it's me don't exist.

It strikes him that all his memories could be false. Who's to say. There's no evidence. Maybe he has made himself up.

He sees a scribbled note. *Popped out for coffee. Let you lie in. Won't be long.* He throws his bag onto the bed and shoves his clothes inside. He has to get a move on.

Why did I bring Anna here? Could've stayed longer.

Carl lobs the gear in the boot of his car. He goes back inside and knocks on the old woman's door.

– Hello, dear.

– I've got ta go.

– Oh.

– This is what I owe ya.

– Thanks, love. Will you be coming back?

– Don't know.

– Well, you take care.

– Thanks. And you. Bye.

In the car, he turns the ignition. A dark figure stands across the road, like a ghoul, watching. He stares at the man as he pulls away. Looks like one of Mick's goons, but he can't be sure.

Slow drive, through the lazy traffic of a seaside town. Carl slows at the lights and sees another man, standing on a street corner, watching him go by. It looks like Mick. He comes to a stop and watches the man watching him in the side mirror. The lights change and he drives away.

Several miles along the coast, he pulls up in another seaside town. Run down, desolate, like any seaside town in this God-forgotten land. Carl finds another guest house. Inside, shabby room. Old décor and thin sheets. He stashes the money on top of the wardrobe and lies on the bed.

The phone lights up, ringing. It's Anna.

– 'Allo

– You alright?

– Yeah.

– Where are you?

– Gone.

– What d'ya mean, gone?

– I'm not there any more.

– Well I know that, I've just seen the old woman. Why? Where are you?

– I don't want you knowin' my whereabouts, do I?

– But I thought you were coming back with me.

– You thought wrong.

– I went out for coffee and a little walk.

– I'm gone.

– Carl, we understand each other.

– I understand nothing.

– Carl, don't do this.

– Goodbye.

He dumps the call and switches it off. Lies there looking at the ceiling.

Down along the beach, a rock wall rises above. Sun low in the wretched sky. Orange disc, pink clouds. Nobody about. Carl passed a dog walker some way back, but now the sand is deserted. A dark arch appears in the rocky wall. A cave. Curious mystery. Carl crouches and goes inside. A passage disappears off into the cold rock. Carl looks back out at the beach through the ragged arch. The sun is setting over the sick sea. He turns back into the cave and switches on his phone for a torch.

A ghostly glow throws light on the moving walls. Carl walks deeper into the cavern. The space is at once tight and infinitely vast. As he sweeps the dim glow of the phone across the walls, he notices chalk-like graffiti. No words, only symbols and pictures. On one wall, a bird-like figure removes the heart of a man. On another, a spectral apparition consumes the heart of a dead man.

Carl moves deeper. He stops abruptly at the vision before him. Flickering light, as though a fire is burning just out of sight. Shadows dance on the wall. The shadows of two humans. One brings a rock down hard on the other's head. The struck figure lies stunned. The standing figure kneels by the prone man and reaches into the torso. A throbbing egg is pulled out and then eaten. Carl sees movement at the far end of the cavern. Solid shapes. People. The flickering light goes out and he is lost in darkness. He tries to get out quick but bangs his head on the rock. His phone is not working. He catches his shin on a low rock and then breaks free of the darkness into the red arch glow of a sunset beach.

WALKING THE SEAFRONT, CARL IS BUMPED ALONG BY THE CROWDS OF people. Faces leer out of the groaning mass. Knowing. Mocking. They sense his fear. Everything is set against him. He understands this. The people in his way, the noise, atmosphere of dread and doom. The watchers, watching. An old man on a bench. A woman at the bus stop. Carl fights his way through the endless herd. The mob. They all move as one. Shrill screams of childish happiness. Angry, impatient parents. A dropped ice cream. Screaming gulls.

He makes it to the cafe, crosses the road and goes inside. Relief of calm quiet. He orders bacon and eggs.

– Don't cut the toast.

– Anything to drink?

– Tea, please.

A newspaper has a front-page article about the gang murders. Police still baffled by the bizarre killings. Increased shootings. A criminal whose identity is protected talks about the paranoia and blame behind the shootings. His breakfast arrives. It looks alright. Nice eggs and decent bacon. He makes a sandwich with the toast. Carl thinks of his brother. They used to do the crossword together in the cafe. He thinks about his predicament and wonders what to do next. He could drift up around the coast and back down the other side. He could move north and settle down. Start again.

He looks up and catches the eye of a small man sitting at the front corner of the cafe. The man is watching him. He has no food, only a mug of tea. Had he heard Carl's thoughts? Carl stares the man down and carries on eating. Every time he looks up, the man is looking at him. He finishes his food and pays at the till.

– Is there a toilet out the back?

– Yes.

– Cheers.

Carl walks through to the back, past the toilet, past the kitchen and out a back door. He comes out on a quiet back street, an access road to the back of the shops. Dirt track for the dust cart and deliveries. He walks back to the busy main road, looks about and keeps walking. The fuss of the mass is eating into his brain. If one more person gets in his way, he's going to knock them down.

A face stands out from the crowd. Mick. Standing across the road, still amongst the moving people. He fades to nothing. Carl quickens his pace. He turns off the promenade and up a side street. He looks behind him and sees Anna standing at the end of the road. Walks faster. Looks back and she's gone. He turns off down another narrow road.

Inside the bedsit, he feels safer. Going outside is becoming more stressful. He avoids it as much as possible during the busy part of the day. It's better in the evening, when the streets are clear and he can find somewhere cheap to eat and stroll along the beach.

He gets out the works and cooks up a dose of peace. Injects himself with serenity, and looking out the window feels the euphoria spread through him.

Carl is chasing a woman through a run-down building. Men are pursuing him too. Shadow men. Carl follows the girl through broken rooms, each more derelict than the last. He tries to see her face, but she never quite looks round at him. The rooms are filthier and more ruined the further he goes. The shadows are closing in. The rooms get darker. The girl is gone, but the men are bearing down on him. He feels a muted sense of panic. Distant. Back in the bedroom briefly. Then he's in a meadow. Looking at the clouds and watching a bird circle the sky. It finds its prey and swoops down. Its shadow gets bigger and spreads out across the field. The bird is a giant. The shadow engulfs him. Swallows him up.

THIS ROOM IS HAUNTED BY ALL THE PEOPLE WHO EVER SLEPT IN IT. All their nightmares. Fears. A collective horror, solid in the air. Again, no sleep. Thoughts racing. Looking out the window. Quiet road, lit by street lamp. Pacing the floor. Sitting on the bed, head in hands. Heartbeat thumping. Goes to the bathroom. Piss loud in the toilet. Shattering the peace of the night. A feeling of someone standing behind him. Up close, breathing down his neck. Carl finishes and spins round. Nobody there.

Back in the room. Potential of everyday objects coming alive, malevolent. He gets dressed, puts his shoes on. Through the door and out into the sharp night. Mad moon in a sad sky. Scene lit by the sick, ethereal glow of a flickering street lamp. Walking with no purpose. Lost. The night-time road is another world. Roaming like a cat. The streets are his. Nobody about. Carl searching for an answer.

And then, as always when you let go, the answer comes: it doesn't matter. None of it. He's got what he wanted. Finished with that business. Done. They won't find him if he don't go back. He can drift through life. Town to town. Mick ain't a young man. He won't last. They'll forget about him. Carl thinks of Anna. He sees her face, smiling. Feels a longing. Want. Lonely. Why did she have to be involved with Mick?

A cat runs under a car. The moon blinks. Strange quiet broken by lazy footsteps scraping on paving stones. The houses are watching. Parked cars, walls and trees have people hiding behind them, waiting to ambush. He is being followed. He looks back and the street is empty. But something lurks in the emptiness.

Down by the sea a deep peace falls over him. The black waves crash. Water laps at the sand. In the darkness, the sound of the sea is all there is. Carl walks along the lonely beach. He stops at the cave. Black arch in the stone wall. He stares into it with the rush and the splash of the sea in his ears. He doesn't go in. Stands looking into the abyss. He has no idea how long he's been standing there. Looks up and down the beach, then walks back along the front.

In his bedroom, he gets undressed. He sits on the bed and looks around. Unease in the furniture. A dripping tap. The whole place buzzes with white noise. Carl cooks a fix and shoots up a slow dream. Lies back on the bed and drifts into delirium.

CARL IS LOOKING AT HIMSELF IN THE MIRROR. THE REFLECTION smiles back at him. Hideous. All wrong. Untold monsters behind that ragged grin. His eyes are holes leading to oblivion. Everything else blurs to obscurity. Vanishes. The eyeballs floating in nothing. They hang framed by the black arch of the cave on a lonely beach. Hole in the cold stone. Carl materialises around the eyes. A voice calls his name. He turns round, facing the back of the cavern. Walks into the gloom.

A loud scraping crashes through the space behind him. He spins round to see an old, dirty room with a small stage. The room is dark. A spotlight shines on the stage with two figures. There is a sunflower and an extraordinary bird circles above. He sees himself with Anna. She is naked on all fours. There is a great tension between them. She looks up at him with love in her eyes. The other him slaps her, grabs her by the back of the neck and forces her face to the floor. She stays like that, with her arse sticking up in the air. The other Carl strokes her. He says, blow me a kiss, and she lets go a fart. He does a little dance.

Carl claps at the dramatic performance as the curtain falls.

The stage drapes rise to the same pair of players, with a muscular beast playing the accordion. Now, Anna is four times the size of the other Carl. The little Carl is a string puppet. She grins as she makes him dance to the music. The beast plays for some time and the little marionette is forced to dance on and on. The music distorts. Carl is mesmerised and lost in the peculiar music. He believes it will never stop. Anna pulls a large pair of scissors from her dress and cuts the strings. The puppet falls dead on the stage.

Carl gives applause as the curtain drops again.

The curtain opens once more to the beast lying on its back, unconscious. Anna walks onstage in a trance with a sharp knife and opens the beast's torso. Reaches inside and pulls out a beating heart. She holds it up to the light, then takes a bite, blood running down her chin. Her eyes are distant, focused on a faraway scene.

Carl cheers as the curtain closes.

A voice behind him calls his name. He turns to find himself on a desolate beach. The waves rise and fall, crash and hiss. A cave in the rocks. Black arch. In the darkness, he sees a beating heart, floating. There is a shell on the sand by his feet. Carl picks it up and holds it to his ear. A scream tears through his skull and he pulls the shell away from his head. Dark cloud moves across the grey above. A shadow spreads out across the beach, a black shape is growing within him.

Lying there on the bed, writhing, twisting. Tangled in sheets wet with sweat. Shivering. Unbearable irritation in the legs and all through him. Prickly heat, and at the same time a chill to the bones. Cold, so cold. Burning up in a fever. He gags on his breath. His stomach knots up with terrible cramps. A sudden surge rushing up to his face and he struggles to get up, swaying. His legs, painful. Creaking bones like an old man.

He makes it just in time, emptying the acrid flow down the bowl. Tears sting his eyes like acid. Heaving. Again and again, wrenching his insides. Like he'd throw up his stomach any moment. Then, lower down, a bubbling pain in the gut. He struggles with his trousers and sits down in time for another torrent below.

Lying in bed, the fever takes him. He falls, sinking into the mattress, the room blurring. The cure, so near to hand, and yet he knows it's the start of a downhill journey. A path he's trodden before. Lost. A game you can't win. He looks at the bag with the cure and sees it move away, far into the distance. It blurs and becomes nothing. Pain in every direction.

He sees Dean's face, lolling, distorted. The noose tight around his neck. He hangs there peacefully. The image beckons Carl and he reaches out to it with his cold, dead hand. Longing to join his poor brother in peace. The face changes and it's his. He watches himself hanging. The vision fades and he is left with nothing.

The pain dissolves him. The breath burns his lungs. He tries to turn, but it feels like the bed is tipping him out and he holds onto the sheets for dear life. He looks up and the ceiling is near, as though the bed has risen. It rocks and bobs as if he is floating. Adrift in nothingness. There's no hope.

He lies there, delirious, kicking his legs and moaning softly. There's nothing else he can do. Anna's face appears before him. Ghostlike. A look of judgement. Then a smile. He'd give anything to have her here now. Mopping his brow, telling him everything will be alright. But he's alone and no one can join him in this nowhere hell. No hope, no hope.

A shadow falls across the room. Everything is silent. The seconds move slow. A space between each tick. Infinity. Time turns in on itself and starts to move backwards. Time horrifies him in a startling realisation that he has to exist day after day after day. He has to keep going 'til the end. How can he keep functioning for so long? He can't take it. Must be a way out sooner. He understands the infinite is different from forever. Forever is a period of time. The infinite is not under any such constraint. When you touch infinity, you touch God. At once, both terror and bliss. Sublime.

THE PHONE RINGS. IT'S JANE. CARL WATCHES THE SCREEN LIT UP WITH her name. The ringing ends. It starts again and he answers.

– Hello.

– Carl. Are you alright?

– Yeah, I'm good. You?

– Not bad.

– Did you sort out things with your boy?

– I've got a meeting next week to talk about supervised visits.

– That's good.

– It's better than nothing. You want to meet up?

– Yeah, but I don't want ta come over there.

– No, that's alright, I'll come to you.

– Yeah, cool.

– Good. I'll be there tomorrow, if that's good for you.

– That's good.

•

Lying in bed together, Carl with his arm around Jane, looking into nothing, while she looks into him. She listens to his breath. They stay like that for some time. Him detached. Her locked in.

– Did you miss me?

– No.

– No?

– I was busy. I been sick.

– What's wrong?

– Don't worry about it. I'm better now.

Carl sees that Jane senses she's not being told the whole story, but she doesn't ask him for any more.

– I missed this.

Carl grabs a handful of flesh and Jane giggles. He gets up and starts putting his clothes on.

– Get dressed. I wanna show you somethin'.

Hand in hand along the beach, and the sea is calm. The small waves roll in and crash on the sand. It is quiet at this time, as the sun sits low. The colour in the clouds changes everything. The golden light reflects off the quicksilver sea. Broken into millions of glittering fragments. It's peaceful.

They come to the cave and Carl steps in.

– In 'ere.

Jane follows. He stops short in front of her, faced with the back of the cave. A stone wall, solid and ancient, stands where passages had led him further in before.

– What's the matter?

– It's different.

– Different to what?

– I don't know. Nothing. It don't matter.

– Is this what you wanted to show me.

– Yeah. No. Forget it.

– Are you alright?

– Yeah.

Carl is quiet as he looks out to sea. Jane stands beside him. She puts her arm round him. He looks behind and their shadows are long on the sand. A cloud drifts across the sky and its shadow moves over the beach towards them. Jane leans her head on his shoulder.

– This is nice.

– Yeah. Come on, let's go.

•

Carl watches her go through the gate and waits 'til she gets to the train. She looks round and waves and then climbs in. He turns and walks out of the station.

Standing at the back of the cave, he looks at the solid rock. He rubs his face. Nothing makes any sense.

Finishing his breakfast in the cafe, Carl looks out the window at the front and sees a man looking in at him. He pays and leaves. The man watches him walk away. As he turns into the side street, Carl sees another man looking at him, eyes following. Carl holds his stare until he turns the corner.

Back in his room. A day impossible to live through. Followed by another, and another. The horror of it seeps into his bones, agitates him. A voice calls his name at his left ear. Pointless. Everything is splintered. Hard to think. Thoughts racing. A powerful beam disrupting his concentration.

He gives up, undresses and goes back to bed. Lies there, holding onto the sheets. Looks at the wardrobe. It leans towards him. He doesn't know what to do with himself. Twisting and turning, afraid of everything. No meaning. No reason. Everything is against him. Lying in bed all day will only make it worse, he knows well enough.

Carl gets up. He looks out the window at the blue sky. The sun is shining. Dressing, he decides to go out. Down at the seafront, he finds a bench and sits in the sun. The sun shines down on him and then hides behind a cloud. The sky turns grey and a dark shape looms. The shadow creeps across the pavement towards him.

A woman walks past and looks at Carl. Her eyes are black. Her stare stabs through him and he is frozen in the glare. The same entity controls all the people, watching him through them.

Walking along the beach, he comes to the cave. Standing there looking at it, but he doesn't go in. He sees, through the dim shade, the back of the cave. Starts laughing. A mother and her children look at him, shocked. It reminds him of a time when he was told of a friend's death. He burst out laughing and everyone looked at him with the same shocked face. He didn't go to the funeral.

As he walks back to his room, everybody is watching him or following him. He tries not to believe it, but it's too strong. He can't ignore it.

Back in the room, he holds a cellophane bag of light brown powder and rolls it in his hand. He presses it with his thumb, feeling the texture. Very fine through the plastic. Puts it back in the drawer, then closes it. Carl opens it again and looks at it. It looks back at him. *Eat me*. Carl cooks it up and injects himself gently. Euphoric warmth in the back of the head, where the skull meets the neck. The room in soft focus now. Everything dissolves in delirium. The off switch is good for the soul. He wonders why he stopped pressing it. Why fight it?

Sean puts the beers down on the small table. It's quiet. A few men drinking round the bar on stools.

– Cheers, mate.

– Cheers.

– So all that gear was knocked off?

– Yeah.

– You're fuckin' crazy.

– Yeah, but he told me to do it and then said he hadn't.

– Why did you ask me to sell it ta Jack? You could 'ave sorted it out with 'em.

– Na. It was a bit too late. Not only that, but I'd had enough. Fuck 'em. They forced me to get back into it and I'm free now. I'm gonna disappear.

– Why didn't you tell me about all this before?

– If I told you that tackle was knocked off, you wouldn't have touched it with a bargepole.

A heavily built man pulls up a low stool and joins them at the table.

– Hello?

– Yes, hello.

– This is a private conversation.

– Yes, yes, I understand. Private.

The man sits there, staring at Carl.

– So, can you go away, please.

The man doesn't move. Sean tries to explain again.

– We're trying to have a private chat.

– Yes yes, private.

Carl starts to get agitated. Psychic attack.

– So fuck off.

The man sits still, eyes boring into Carl. The bar gets smaller around them. Carl stands up. Angry.

– Fuck off, or I'm gonna knock you out.

The man smiles.

– I sit and you angry, yes yes.

Carl leans over and punches him in the side of the head. The big man goes down, tipping out of his seat. He stays on the floor, holding a hand to his temple. Carl picks up his pint and takes a long drink. Several men at the bar come over.

– Leave it out.

– Why did you hit him?

– We don't want no trouble in 'ere.

Carl glares at them.

– Come on, let's get out of 'ere.

He struts out. Thrilled with the win. He looks up and down the street. Everything is his. He feels the power flow through his veins. Nothing can stop him. Sean comes out behind him.

– Are you alright, mate?

– Yeah, I am now.

They walk down the road.

– Why did you hit 'im?

– He was trying to get into my head.

– What d'ya mean?

– He was gonna start trouble.

– But he was just sitting there.

– If I hadn't of hit 'im, he'd have hit me. I'm tellin' ya.

– Let's find another pub.

They walk along the road. There are several pubs along the way.

– What about in 'ere?

They walk into the quiet bar, old man's pub. Like walking into another time. Two old boys at the bar, one sitting alone at a table. They look up as the two men enter. Carl buys a couple of pints.

– So what are you goin' ta do?

– Dunno. Float about a bit, I reckon. I might pay 'em back eventually. Sort things out if I can. I got enough dough ta be getting on with 'til then. Apart from what I ripped off them, I got me own bit saved up 'n all.

– What happened to that bird you used ta see?

– What, Anna?

– Yeah.

– I was still seeing her on and off.

– Oh yeah?

– She works with them lot, don't she.

– Oh right.

– Yeah.

TREVOR LYING IN BED. CLEAN WHITE SHEETS. SMELL OF DISINFECTANT. The ward is busy around him, but he sleeps through the noise. Visiting times bring him few visitors. He was never a popular man. The curtain is pulled around his bed. He sleeps as the heavy hammer smashes into his skull. Dull thud unheard. The nurses are all occupied. He opens up to The Hunter. His heart is released, beating. The Hunter bites into it and eats it all. The Hunter sharply sucks in air and exhales a long, heavy breath, as its halo burns bright. Blood pools on the bed and drips down to the floor.

Nobody notices the creature leave any more than they noticed it arrive.

THERE ARE MANY CARLS. THEY GO ON FOREVER, ONE AFTER ANOTHER. Infinite Carls. Some of them are looking at each other. They all move as one. Carl makes his way through the mirrored maze. He touches his face in the glass ahead. There's movement behind him and he sees a dark figure with a grinning head creep up on him. He spins round to face it, but there's no one there. He listens to the silence. Standing dead still, watching himself. A ridiculous moment.

Round another corner, he sees the face again, but it fades to shadow as he focuses on it in the reflection. Cold fear sweeps through him as he feels his way around the glass walls. Why did he come in here? He sees his own movement reflected endlessly. A shadow moves behind him. There's only one way out. He can't go back to the beginning. He's come too far. He keeps on moving through the maze. He catches his reflection grinning at him.

– What are you smilin' at?

Carl watches himself say the words and nothing seems real. It's like he's watching a character on the telly. He laughs and it sounds fake. A thousand Carls laugh back.

A group of people enter the maze behind him. Their voices echo round the mirrored walls. Carl finds the exit and the daylight is too bright. He makes his way into an absurd afternoon.

•

The promenade is alive with cries of excitement and people everywhere. There are stalls selling T-shirts, souvenirs and street food. As he walks through the crowded street, Carl sees a girl in a polka-dot dress. Anna. The girl is standing twenty or so metres away from him. He stops and stares at her. She has her back to him. He can't see her face, but he is sure it is her. He pushes through the crowd, but the flow of people is against him and the further he goes, the further away she seems to be. People pushing past. A fat woman bumps into him and blocks his way. He tries to go round her, but he nearly falls over her children. When he looks up, the girl in the polka-dot dress is gone.

Carl pushes on and catches a glimpse of her dress in the distance. An ugly, red-faced man gets up in his face and shouts at Carl to stop pushing, but he is focused on trying to catch up with the girl. It is Anna, he is sure. He sees her disappear between shops up an alley. Keeps on pushing through the waves of people. There she is again, further up the street. A girl in a pink tutu and leotard bends over in front of him. There is a space cleared around her and Carl goes to cross it, but she leaps into his path and begins to dance. Graceful limbs. She salutes and pirouettes, prances this way and that, and every time he tries to go, she shimmies in his direction. People begin to laugh at her game and he grows more frustrated at every turn. The crowd are all pointing and laughing at him. Everyone against him. He manages to feign a move and she spins that way and he sidesteps her and gets away.

Where is his Anna? Where is his polka-dot girl? He looks through the throng and sees the girl swallowed up in the mob. As he looks back angrily at the ballerina and her audience, he sees Mick following him with two thugs. Adrenaline poisons the blood. He pushes into the crowd. Ugly faces and so much noise. Carl presses on.

A man in scruffy clothes, like a tramp with a white face, big red lips and black eyes, leans in his way and sticks his tongue out. Another shabby man with red curly hair sticking out from beneath a blue bowler hat, black lips, a red nose and yellow cheeks, juggles sticks of fire. A third man with a blue face leaps around, backflips and dances in an apish fashion. The crowd clap and cheer around them. Carl gets away from them and keeps going.

He looks up the street to see a quick flash of the polka-dot girl, before she again disappears in the mass. Looking back and the three ominous thugs are still following. He is sure one of them is Mick. His polka-dot girl is there, standing still, ahead of him. Anna. She is looking away to the sea. As he watches, the wind catches the hem at the back of her dress. It flutters, teasing at the top of her thighs, then blows right up and he sees her beautiful bare cheeks. Carl is mesmerised as the dress blows around her waist. She doesn't notice or doesn't care. It's his Anna.

The stalls are busy, and the queues of people have blocked the pavements and spill out onto the road. It is almost impossible to squeeze through. He pushes and dodges and works his way along. Carl loses sight of the polka-dot girl, but he keeps going. He looks behind and the three thugs are catching up. The crowd parts for them and the polka-dot girl, but close down on him like an impenetrable force.

As he gets past a queue of people crowded round a stall, he is blocked once again, by three men on stilts. The high men tilt and step around him. Each way he turns, he is blocked by a long leg. He pushes back through the crowds and comes face to face with a mime. Every move he makes is aped by the mime artist and the audience laugh, until with building anger, Carl shoves the man out of the way and the crowd boos. He's pushed and shoved as he goes.

As he pushes through the bustle, the mob move as one to block him and stall him in every direction. Heavyset men still like rock, fat men and women waddle in the way, small children trip him over. Skinny men and women dart in front of him, thrown mischievously in his path.

He can no longer see the polka-dot girl. He looks around frantically. So many people. Where is she? He must find her. He's sure it was her. Looking behind him, the three thugs are gone. As he turns back, he knocks into a vicious-faced man with a group of young villains. Looking for trouble. The man shoves Carl in the chest.

– Watch where you're goin'.

– Fuck off.

The yobs surround Carl, pushing and shoving, trying to intimidate. Carl lashes out and punches a skinny one in the face. They all lay into him, kicking and punching. People are trying to get out of the way. He manages to get away through the crowd and makes a run for the beach. They chase him down the concrete steps and onto the sand. The beach is crowded. Carl runs on the uneven sand, dodging people lying on towels, holes dug out by children and sandcastles, buckets and spades. The men run him down and catch him in a small clearing on the beach. He punches and kicks, but he's soon overwhelmed. He goes down. They beat him into the sand. He gives up and lies there as the kicks and stamps rain down.

Eventually, they lose interest and leave him. Nobody offers their help. He lies for a while with his eyes closed, listening to the waves crash on the shore and the children playing and the screaming gulls. He can't be bothered to move, and he thinks he could lie there for ever. The red light on the back of his eyelids turns black and he looks up to see an old man bending over him.

– Are you alright, son?

– Yeah.

– Do you want a hand getting up?

– No. I'm gonna lie here a bit.

– Do you want me to call the police, or an ambulance?

– No. I'm alright. I just want to lie here for a while.

– Alright. I'll leave you alone then.

The old man looks at some people sitting nearby and shrugs, then walks away.

Carl looks up at the sky. There is sand in his jeans and socks. One of his shoes has come off. A cloud moves across the blue and a shadow crawls along the beach towards him.

CARL CLIMBS THE STAIRS TO THE LANDING. THE STAIRWAY IS DARK with a little light diffused through the frosted glass in the bathroom door. He is startled at the top step and stiffens in surprise. His brother is hanging from the loft hatch. Dean turns gently. His face is blank, as if he's been waiting and is bored with hanging there.

– How you been?

Dean's voice is flat and emotionless. He talks like it's any other normal day.

– I'm alright. Not the best.

– You gotta hold it down, brother.

– I know, but I'm struggling.

– You gotta hold it together.

– Well, this ain't exactly helping.

– All these monsters, they're from within you.

– Everything is against me.

– It's you, bruv. You're fightin' your own self.

– I'll be alright. It'll all be alright in the end.

– That's the spirit. Chin up. Shoulders back. Stand tall.

– How are you?

– Me? I'm dead, ain't I. It's alright.

– What's it like?

– A lot fuckin' easier than being alive.

– Oh. Good. I might join ya.

– Na. You keep goin'. You're gonna die anyway. Might as well make the most of it while you're here.

– Yeah. I just can't be bothered with the pain.

– It's too bad.

Carl walks round his hanging brother and opens the door to his room.

– See you later, mate.

– Yeah. Take it easy.

He closes the door behind him. The room is still and quiet. Carl puts the kettle on and sits down on the end of the bed. Head in hands, he thinks about Anna. He misses her. Takes a long hit from the bottle of whisky and puts it back on the sideboard.

CARL LIES ON THE BED STARING AT THE CEILING. UNDER ATTACK FROM his own thoughts. Are they his? They come so fast, he can't think straight. They must be alien thoughts, projected into his mind by an external entity. A control box. Mind machine. He tries to concentrate. To see through them. He attempts to hold on to one thought. One memory.

He had a goldfish when he was a boy. Won it from a fair. His mother had put it in a small glass bowl and it lived there on the windowsill. The fish got neglected. Someone would remember to feed it every now and then, and he wondered how it didn't die of starvation. The bowl was rarely cleaned out and the water turned green with filth.

The fish stayed alive for years. It went on and on. Nobody could believe it. No one cared. Carl tried to remember how long that fish had lasted. Eight years. Ten maybe. It was a long time. It died some time in his late teens. He wondered how it survived. Why? Swimming round and round in its own shit in that small bowl. How did it not just give up?

Carl had wanted to give up. To just fall down and die. Many times. But he kept going too. Why? He realises the alien thoughts have stopped. Lying there, staring at the ceiling, he thinks about that fish. He sees it swimming round in the green water. His brother was right. He can't give up. He has to stay alive. Things aren't so bad now for him. He's free. He can do what he wants. Nothing matters.

– WE JUST WANT YOU TO RING HIM. TELL HIM TO MEET YOU. When he gets there, you can leave.

Jane looks from Anna to Mick. She doesn't respond. Mick leans forward and strokes her face, then gently closes his hand around her throat.

– Listen, ya little tart. You know who I am?

The frightened girl nods.

– So you're gonna ring 'im, or you're gonna get your teeth knocked in, ain't ya? Now, do I 'ave ta find your little boy, or are you gonna play nice?

She nods again. Mick lets go of her neck and strokes her cheek.

– I'm off. Sort this slut out. I'll talk to you later. She'd look nice dancing at the club.

– Maybe. See you later.

Anna turns back to Jane and watches her cry for a moment, then strokes her hair.

– Don't cry. It'll be alright, I promise. He won't get hurt. I'll make sure of it. I want him safe too. He's got something we want, that's all.

Tears fall down Jane's cheeks.

– I know you was fuckin' him, but he's mine. Do you understand?

Jane looks at Anna, afraid.

– You're lucky I don't give you a slapping for that. Just be a good girl and do as we say. It'll all work out. Yeah?

– Yeah.

– Good girl.

THERE IS A LOW MIST AND IT'S HARD TO SEE. THE FOG ENVELOPS the old foundries in a mystic cloud. The industrial estate is derelict. Weeds growing up through the cracked concrete. Quiet. A feeling of being watched. Abandoned warehouses in a sad dream. Why did she want to meet here? Carl walks to a desolate blue building. Looks about. No one there. He goes up a small flight of concrete steps to a black, wooden door in the side of the building. As he puts his hand on the door handle, a feeling of poison in the blood. It feels wrong. Bleak foreboding. He is a scared child in the dark. He pauses like that for a while before trying the door. It opens.

Inside the big, empty room, Jane is standing in the middle, lit from a high window. She looks odd in the vast space. Awkward. Out of place. Blatant bait.

– Alright?

His voice echoes through the silence. He walks to where she stands. Footsteps crunch on the cold concrete floor. Sad eyes. Jane looks like she's been crying.

– What's the matter?

– I'm sorry.

There is movement in the darkness behind her. Mick and Anna appear by a door to an office. Mick grinning, monstrous face, Anna looking through him and far away. Carl turns round to see a heavily built man at the door he'd entered through. Mick laughs. Jane looks at her feet. Anna's eyes are blank.

– You can fuck off now.

Jane can't look at Carl. She walks to the door where the thug stands guard and squeezes past him to leave.

– Come here, son.

Mick sounds calm. Carl walks to the office. Loud steps. As he crosses the floor, time slows down and it takes a while to get across the emptiness between them. He goes through the door, past Mick, following Anna to a big desk with chairs. Mick calls out to the big man at the door.

– You might as well go 'n all. I don't need you now. Make sure she's not hangin' about.

The man goes out and pulls the door behind him. It slams and echoes through the building.

Carl stands in the office staring at Anna. She is right there in front of him and so far away. Her expression is unreadable. He wonders what she's getting out of it. His vision turns black as a big bang explodes behind him and Carl finds himself on the floor. He realises Mick has punched him in the back of the head. He pulls himself up and leans on a chair. Anna says nothing. A wave of nausea goes through him and his legs feel weak.

– Siddown.

Carl sits, holding his head. Mick goes to stand behind the desk with Anna.

– So, you thought you'd do off with my gear, did ya?

Carl stays quiet, looking at the floor.

– Did you think you could run forever?

Carl rubs the back of his head and starts to laugh. Carnival laugh of a madman doomed.

– I'm talkin' ta you. Are you fuckin' listening?

Carl looks up at Anna, a blank expression with no care, no emotion. He becomes aware of a great power emanating from within her. A visible pulsing. Her eyes light up and burn. Mick turns away to suppress a rising anger as the violence builds within him. Violence and chaos build in the room. A bright light shines out from Anna. She has a halo. Carl's eyes are locked on hers.

Carl feels a lurch in his gut like the world fell away and he drops. Spinning rush. The room breathes and ripples around them. Time stops. The wall behind them swells and shrinks. Bulges out like a bubble. Dean rises from the burning floor, maniac grin caught in a beam of light from the single window. Spectral faces hang in the air, screaming. A hand grabs a stone paperweight from the desk and swings. Crashes into Mick's temple. Mick goes down, a sharp thud as his face bounces off the corner of the desk. Carl and Anna kissing. Carl watching it all, laughing. The Hunter bears down on the prey. Scream. Quick hands work at clothing, pulling away. A naked girl, dancing. Blood everywhere. Dripping. Running down the walls. Wings flapping. A naked warrior lies ready. Carl falling, tumbling down. Sharp knife opens the trunk. Noise like children laughing fills the room. The beating heart is pulled free and held up to the dim light. Carl sees The Hunter bite into it, glowing. A bird's head. Black feathers and beak. The shining figure becomes Dean, then Carl, and then Anna, blood running down her chin. Carl pulls Anna across the desk and shoves her dress up. Kisses smear the blood across their faces. She opens his jeans. They go at each other in the mess and the gore as the power floods through their veins. The room beats around them.

ACKNOWLEDGEMENTS

Thank you to Arts Council England for awarding me a DYCP grant to write this book.

Thank you to Influx Press and particularly Gary Budden for taking this book on and making a good job of it.

Thanks to Eva Lewin, and everyone else who read this book at various stages and gave encouragement.

Thanks also to my ever-patient wife, Elena.

ABOUT THE AUTHOR

Rob True was born in 1971. Unable to read or write very well, he left school with no qualifications. His wife taught him how to use paragraphs and punctuation aged forty and he began writing stories.

His work has been published in *The Arsonist Magazine, Open Pen, Low Light Magazine, Occulum,* and *Litro Magazine.* His first book, *Gospel of Aberration* was published by Burning House Press.

INFLUX
PRESS

Influx Press is an independent publisher based in London, committed to publishing innovative and challenging literature from across the UK and beyond.

Lifetime supporters: Bob West and Barbara Richards

www.influxpress.com
@Influxpress